BAD. BLUE. BRILLIANT.

THE NOVEL

PRICE STERN SLOAN
Published by the Penguin Group
Penguin Group (USA) Inc., 375 Hudson Street, New York, New York 10014, USA
Penguin Group (Canada), 90 Eglinton Avenue East, Suite 700, Toronto,
Ontario M4P 2Y3, Canada (a division of Pearson Penguin Canada Inc.)
Penguin Books Ltd., 80 Strand, London WC2R 0RL, England
Penguin Group Ireland, 25 St. Stephen's Green, Dublin 2, Ireland
(a division of Penguin Books Ltd.)
Penguin Group (Australia), 250 Camberwell Road, Camberwell, Victoria 3124, Australia
(a division of Pearson Australia Group Pty. Ltd.)
Penguin Books India Pvt. Ltd., 11 Community Centre, Panchsheel Park,
New Delhi—110 017, India
Penguin Group (NZ), 67 Apollo Drive, Rosedale, North Shore 0632, New Zealand
(a division of Pearson New Zealand Ltd.)
Penguin Books (South Africa) (Pty.) Ltd., 24 Sturdee Avenue, Rosebank,
Johannesburg 2196, South Africa

Penguin Books Ltd., Registered Offices: 80 Strand, London WC2R 0RL, England

Library of Congress Cataloging-in-Publication Data is available.

ISBN 978-0-8431-9921-5   10 9 8 7 6 5 4 3 2 1

BAD. BLUE. BRILLIANT.

THE NOVEL

by Lauren Alexander

PSS!
PRICE STERN SLOAN

An Imprint of Penguin Group (USA) Inc.

PROLOGUE

I've always believed that destiny chooses our path in life. There's the path of evil, and the path of good. Now, let me introduce you to the face of pure evil—yours truly, me: Megamind.

I know what you're thinking: How can someone as cute as me be so evil? Do not let my cuteness fool you.

But, I'm getting ahead of myself. Let me tell you my story.

I had a fairly standard childhood. I was born on a blue planet to a blue mother and a blue father. And when I was a mere eight days old, my life as I knew it was completely destroyed. Pretty normal so far, right?

Our planet was in a state of chaos—buildings were collapsing and people were screaming and literally running for their lives as two of our neighboring planets were being sucked into a black hole.

My parents, who couldn't wait to get me out of the house, strapped me into an escape pod. I was all alone, except for my trusty sidekick, Minion. He was a little fish in a fluid-filled ball. My mother promised he'd take care of me. My father threw in my Binky—for comfort, I guess. And with his parting words, he told me that I was destined for greatness. That was a lot of expectation to place on a little baby, don't you think?

Nonetheless, I accepted the challenge with open arms—the arms I reached out for my parents with. But there was no time to be sentimental. They pushed me into my seat in the pod and sent me on my way. I was the last survivor of a doomed planet.

As my pod launched into space, I was alone. Or so I thought.

It turns out that another family from another doomed planet in the Glaupunk Quadrant had a very similar idea. They, too, placed their infant son in a pod and sent him off to safety. As I looked out the window of my pod, I saw the Golden Baby staring back at me through the window of his golden pod. Well, he wasn't just staring— the little brat was sticking his tongue out at me! Mr. Goody-Two-Shoes and I were officially introduced, and our rivalry was born!

Our pods raced toward Earth. Mine was a bumpy ride through an asteroid field. Golden Boy's ride was smooth sailing. My pod hit an orbiting satellite, and was headed toward a palatial estate. Boy, that place sure looked sweet! But then suddenly, the golden pod knocked me off course, and it landed there instead of me! Beautiful gates opened and the golden pod rolled across a stately lawn, through an ornate front door, and came to rest safely under a Christmas tree in the home of Lord and Lady Scott.

And me? My pod tumbled out of the sky, bounced through a dirty alley, and slammed through the wall of the Metro City penitentiary. Instead of a palace, I had landed in jail! But don't feel sorry for me, it was a lovely place, and I called it home.

The prisoners greeted me with open arms. And they taught me many valuable lessons. For instance, they taught me the difference between right—a robber—and wrong—a cop. Simple lessons, really.

Mr. Goody-Two-Shoes, on the other hand, had life handed to him on a silver platter. On that Christmas morning, after the golden pod landed under the tree, Lady Scott thanked her husband for the lovely gift—a baby. Thinking fast, Lord Scott accepted the thanks (really, he had no idea where the baby had come from) and the two became a family of three.

Now, coming from another planet, Mr. Goody-Two-Shoes had superpowers. He had the power of flight, invulnerability, and great hair. I might not have had all the things my rival had, but I did have amazing intellect and a knack for building objects of mayhem. Once I built a tricycle made entirely out of license plates. I rode that toy around the yard, and straight through the prison wall. But I didn't get far; the prison guards caught me and dragged me back to my cell. I learned that the road to success has many obstacles—like barbed wire and laws.

Oh yes, my friends, life is not easy when you're young and blue. When I came of school-age, I had to have a special escort (a police officer) wait with me for the school bus. And when I arrived at school wearing my first-day-of-school outfit (an orange jumpsuit), I ran into my old traveling companion, Mr. Goody-Two-Shoes. He had already amassed a gigantic army of soft-headed groupies, easily fascinated by his "godlike" powers. When he saw me enter the classroom, he pointed at me and laughed. The rest of the kids laughed along. So, you see, fitting in wasn't really an option. I had no choice but to strike back with devastating fury. It was then I decided to embrace evil to achieve greatness.

As a schoolboy, I learned a very hard lesson—good (Mr. Goody-Two-Shoes) receives all the praise and gold stars, while evil (me) is sent to quiet time in the corner. Sitting in that corner, I spotted two bottles labeled Do Not Mix. A lightbulb went off in my head. Are you having a hard time following me? I'll put it to you simply—I blew up the school!

Through those childhood years, one man always stood in my way. Our battles quickly got more elaborate. He would win some. I would almost win others.

And then she came into our lives.

The "she" I'm talking about is none other than Roxanne Ritchi, nosy reporter. And the closest thing to a weakness my adversary had. He took the name of Metro Man: Defender of Metro City. While

I was in prison, I decided to pick something a little more humble—
Megamind: Incredibly Handsome Criminal Genius and Master of
All Villainy. And this, my friends, is our story . . .

CHAPTER ONE

Megamind grew up to be a real villain inside that prison. He was so evil and so cunning that he was locked up under special security.

One day, the warden came to check up on Megamind in his cell. A guard pressed a button, and the warden spoke to Megamind through an observation window. It wasn't safe to get any closer to the villain, who was strapped to a chair.

"Still working on your autobiography?" the warden asked.

"Editing, actually," Megamind replied. "I want to get it down to a breezy nine hundred pages. You know, for kids."

The warden shook his head. "You sicko."

"It's part of my rehabilitation," Megamind said with

a smile. "I'm a changed man, and I'm ready to reenter society as a solid citizen."

"You're a villain, and you'll always be a villain. You'll never change, and you'll never leave," the warden informed him.

"You're fun," Megamind said, not taking his comments too seriously.

The warden picked up a box. "You got a present in the mail."

"Is it a pickax?" Megamind asked.

The warden ignored Megamind and unwrapped the box. Inside was a gold watch with a note attached.

"From Metro Man, 'To count every second of your eighty-five life sentences,'" the warden read. "That's funny. Never thought Metro Man was the gloating type."

The warden turned the watch over in his hands, then slipped it on his wrist. It was way too nice to waste on the likes of Megamind.

"He does have nice taste," the warden said, admiring the watch. "I think I'll keep it." And with that, he turned to leave.

"Oh, Warden," Megamind called after him. "Any chance you could give me the time? I don't want to be late for the opening of the Metro Man Museum."

"Looks like you're going to miss it," the warden snorted. "By several thousand years." He turned on his heels and left.

"Oh, am I?" Megamind said with a sinister laugh. The villain had a plan up his sleeve, and it was about to unfold.

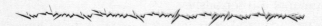

Meanwhile, everyone in Metro City was getting ready to honor their biggest hero, Metro Man, with the opening of the Metro Man Museum.

"It's a beautiful day in beautiful downtown, where we are here to honor a beautiful man," reporter Roxanne Ritchi said into a microphone.

"For years he's been watching us with his super vision, saving us with his superstrength, and caring for us with his super heart," Roxanne said into the camera. "Now it's our turn to give something back. This is Roxanne Ritchi, reporting live from the dedication of the Metro Man Museum."

The cameraman switched off the camera. "Wow, the stuff they make you read on-air. That's unbelievable. It's crazy!" he said.

"I wrote that piece myself, Hal," Roxanne told him.

Quickly, Hal tried to cover up. "What I was trying to say was, I can't believe that in our modern society they let, like, actual art get onto the news."

"Not sure I'm following," Roxanne said, puzzled.

Hal tried to change the subject and suggested that they grab a cup of coffee. But Roxanne didn't want to hide out in a coffee shop somewhere. It was Metro Man's big day, and it was time to celebrate. She tried to get Hal into the spirit.

But Hal didn't think Metro Man was such a big deal. "If I were Metro Man, Megamind wouldn't be grabbing you all the time," Hal told her, remembering the countless times the villain had kidnapped the reporter.

"That's sweet, Hal," Roxanne said with a smile.

"And I'd be watching you. Like a dingo watches a human baby," Hal continued.

Roxanne looked puzzled again.

"Okay, that sounded a little weird," Hal admitted.

"A little bit, yeah," Roxanne agreed.

"And you're making a weird face and that's making me feel weird," Hal said, wandering away from her.

Roxanne stared after the cameraman and shook her head. That guy sure was strange.

Then an invisible car pulled up next to her. In an

instant, a robotic gorilla arm reached out with an aerosol can and sprayed her in the face. Roxanne fell through the car's open window, and a hood was slipped over her head. Then, just as fast as the car had appeared, it sped off into the distance.

Oblivious to what had just occurred, Hal was still jabbering on and on. "The point is, I would watch you like something that watches something intently with love. Not love. We're not in love. I'm not saying I love you. I'm saying . . ." Hal's words drifted off as he turned back toward where Roxanne was standing. She was gone!

"Roxanne," Hal called. "Roxerroo?"

But Roxanne Ritchi was nowhere to be seen.

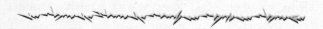

Back inside the cellblock, the warden was walking down the corridor. Suddenly, his new watch began to beep. Was it some sort of alarm? No! The watch face slid open, and a miniature scanner appeared. With a flash of light, the warden was transformed into a perfect likeness of Megamind!

Not knowing what had just happened, the warden continued his stroll down the hall. "Get back to work," he said to two guards who were playing cards with a prisoner. "The city doesn't pay you to loaf."

The guards looked up and were shocked to see Megamind standing before them. Quickly, they drew their guns.

"Whoa, what are you doing?" the warden asked, still not realizing that he had been changed into the villain. "It's me, the warden!" he insisted.

The guards grabbed him, and dragged him off to Megamind's cellblock. Once inside, they strapped him to his chair. As the guards turned to go, the real Megamind, who was hiding behind the chair, reached around and slipped the watch off the warden's wrist. Instantly, the warden turned back into himself.

"You fools," the warden cried to the guards, "he tricked us again!"

The guards looked up and saw the real Megamind at the door.

"You were right," Megamind gloated. "I'll always be a villain."

And with that, he turned the dial on the watch's disguise generator and transformed into the warden. Wiggling his eyebrows, Megamind (as the warden) stepped through the cell door, shutting it behind him and trapping the warden and the guards inside.

Out in the hall, Megamind pulled a lever and the doors to all the cells flew open. It was a chaotic scene as the prisoners fled their cells. But Megamind remained calm as he walked through the prison gates to freedom!

CHAPTER TWO

As Megamind stepped outside the prison gates, the invisible car pulled up in front of him. The door swung open and Megamind smiled at the eight-hundred-pound robotic gorilla, with a fish in a fishbowl for a head, sitting behind the steering wheel. It was Megamind's sidekick, Minion, and he was all grown up!

"Well, hello, good looking. Need a lift?" Minion asked Megamind.

"I certainly do, you fantastic fish, you!" Megamind said as he opened the car door and climbed inside. Once safely inside the invisible car, Megamind flipped a switch on his watch and his warden disguise disappeared.

"I'm free! I'm free!" Megamind shouted for joy. "Nice work sending me the watch, Minion," he told his sidekick.

"You got it, boss," Minion responded as he drove the

car dangerously through traffic.

Megamind then turned to look at Roxanne Ritchi, who was still passed out on the backseat. "And Miss Ritchi," he said even though he knew she couldn't hear him, "I'm glad you could join us for my brand-new plan. We are going to defeat Metro Man, and then, guess what? We're going to rule Metrocity!" Megamind and Minion cheered.

"Now, won't you join me in some maniacal laughter?" Megamind asked his sidekick.

The two laughed as Minion hit the gas and weaved the car through traffic—going the wrong way, of course!

After making their way through town, they finally arrived at a warehouse—Megamind's top secret headquarters. A door slid open and the invisible car drove through. Once inside, the car became visible, and Megamind and Minion, carrying Roxanne, stepped out. Brainbots, Megamind's little robotic creatures, immediately swarmed around him, changing his prison uniform into a splendid villain outfit and cape. Megamind was glad to be rid of his prison gear. The cape was much more him. Nodding to his trusty sidekick, they stepped onto the platform that was next to them. Minion pulled a lever and the platform started to rise to the second floor of the warehouse. The two looked at each other and cracked up.

When they reached the top, Megamind and Minion were out of breath from all the laughing. Suddenly, they heard Roxanne's voice.

"She's awake!" Megamind cried. "To work!"

Quickly, Minion tied Roxanne to a chair. Megamind hopped into another chair, smoothed his eyebrows, and petted the Brainbot that had flown into his lap. He was ready for his big moment. Minion yanked off Roxanne's hood as Megamind slowly turned in his chair to face the reporter.

"Miss Ritchi," Megamind said, "we meet again."

"Oh, it's only you," Roxanne said, clearly unimpressed.

"You can scream all you wish, Miss Ritchi! I'm afraid no one can hear you," Megamind said.

Megamind waited for a minute, but all he heard was silence. "Why isn't she screaming?" he whispered to Minion.

"Miss Ritchi, if you don't mind." Minion tried to get her to scream.

"Like this: *Ahhh!*" Megamind demonstrated. "But that, that's a poor lady scream," he added.

Suddenly, Megamind's Brainbot chomped down on

his hand. Megamind let out a scream—a real one!

"That's a little better," Roxanne commented, looking around at her surroundings. "Is there some kind of nerdy super-villain website where you get Tesla coils and blinky dials?" she asked, referring to all the gadgets hanging around her.

"Actually," Minion began, "most of it comes from an outlet store in—"

"Don't answer that!" Megamind cut him off.

"Romania," Minion whispered.

"Stop," Megamind cautioned. "She's using her nosy reporter skills to find out all our secrets."

"What secrets?" Roxanne scoffed. "You're so predictable."

Megamind was outraged. "Predictable? Predictable? Oh, you call *this* predictable?"

Megamind pushed a button and the floor around Roxanne opened up, revealing a pit of snapping alligators.

Roxanne yawned. "Alligators, yes. I was thinking about it on the way over."

Megamind tried again and again to prove to her that he was definitely *not* predictable. But when a gun flipped out of the wall and pointed straight at her, Roxanne just thought it was cliché. And she declared the rest of the deadly weapons juvenile, tacky, and garish. Roxanne had clearly seen it all. Nothing that Megamind did could impress—or scare—her.

Frustrated, Megamind leaned against a control panel.

"Okay," Roxanne admitted. "The spider is new."

"Spider?" Megamind asked in surprise. He turned to see a spider dangling in front of Roxanne.

"Yes, the . . . spee-ider," Megamind said, clearly improvising. "Even the smallest bite from *arachnus deathicus* will instantly paralyze you."

Not scared a bit, Roxanne blew on the spider.

It landed in Megamind's eye, and he let out a scream. Trying to get his boss under control, Minion slapped Megamind across his face.

"Get it off!" Megamind complained. "*Ow!* It bit me!"

Roxanne sighed. "Give it up, Megamind. Your plans never work."

"Let's stop wasting time and call your boyfriend in tights, shall we?" Megamind suggested.

Roxanne shook her head. She knew where her "boyfriend" was right now—he was in front of the Metro Man Museum greeting his adoring fans. She could just picture the scene.

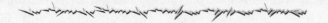

Across town, the mayor of Metro City addressed a giant crowd. "It is with great pleasure that I present to Metro Man this new museum."

Metro Man focused his eyes on the ribbon that was draped in front of the museum's entrance. And with his supersonic heat vision, he cut the ribbon in half! Instantly, a multistory curtain dropped, revealing a towering statue of Metro Man holding a globe.

The crowd went wild. Everyone loved Metro Man. Well, not exactly everyone. Somewhere in the crowd, a figure in a trench coat loomed. It strained its body upward to catch a glimpse of the man everyone else called their hero.

"Hey, my kid can't see," a man said, tapping the figure on its shoulder.

The figure turned. The man was stunned. This wasn't a human blocking his view—it was a Brainbot disguised in a trench coat and hat! And this Brainbot wasn't the only one there. The crowd was swarming with them!

Before the man had a chance to react, dark smoke rolled in from behind the museum. The Brainbots in the crowd raced to the front to project their sinister message.

Megamind's evil laughter filled the air as his image was broadcast onto the walls of the museum.

"Oh, bravo, Metro Man," Megamind congratulated his rival.

The crowd erupted in boos.

"Boo! Yes, I can play along, too," Megamind shot back. "Boo. Does it make you feel better?"

Metro Man shook his head. "Should have known you'd try to crash the party."

"Oh, I intend to do more than crash it. This is a day you and Metrocity shall not soon forget."

"It's pronounced Metro City," Metro Man said, pausing between each word.

Megamind was getting annoyed. "Oh, potato, tomato, po-tah-to, toe-mah-to."

"We all know how this ends—with you behind bars," Metro Man said.

"Oh, I'm shaking in my custom, baby seal, leather boots," Megamind shot back. "You will leave Metrocity or this will be the last you ever hear of Roxanne Ritchi."

Megamind pressed a button and an image of Roxanne tied to her chair was projected on the wall.

"Roxanne!" Metro Man shouted. "Don't panic, Roxie. I'm on my way."

"Yeah, I'm not panicking," Roxanne said calmly.

"In order to stop me, you need to find me first, Metro Man," Megamind challenged.

"We're at the abandoned observatory!" Roxanne shouted out.

Quickly, Megamind cut off her transmission. "No, we're not," he retorted. "Don't listen to her, she's crazy."

Thinking he had a good clue, Metro Man grinned and took off into the air. Scanning the horizon, he spotted the old observatory and raced toward it, determined to save the day yet again.

CHAPTER THREE

"Metro Man approaching, sir," Minion reported, looking up from the computer screen.

"Ha!" Roxanne shouted, pleased that the hero was coming to her rescue.

"Ha! Ha!" Megamind laughed back at her. Clearly, he had something up his sleeve.

Roxanne, Megamind, and Minion watched on the computer screen as Metro Man raced straight toward the telescope that sat on top of the observatory. Landing, he punched through the telescope and walked into the observatory.

Wait a minute, Roxanne wondered. Why hadn't she heard a crash? The telescope was right above her and it remained untouched. She looked back at the screen. The doors to the observatory slammed shut behind Metro

Man. He looked around, confused. There was no one in sight.

Megamind pressed a button and giant metal doors slid apart. Roxanne could see the *real* Metro City Observatory in the distance. She looked up at Megamind.

"Oh, good heavens," Megamind said with a wave of his hand. "You didn't think you were in the *real* observatory, did you?"

For the first time, Roxanne Ritchi was surprised, and a bit scared, too.

"Ready the Death Ray, Minion," Megamind ordered.

"Death Ray ready-ing," Minion reported.

Up in the sky, a sinister-looking satellite orbited Earth. A set of doors on the satellite opened, revealing two huge solar panels. From his position, Minion pulled a lever, and the panels began to charge.

Just then, a giant screen turned on inside the real observatory, where Metro Man was standing. Megamind's image filled the screen.

"Over here, old friend," Megamind called, trying to get the hero's attention. "In case you haven't noticed, you've fallen right into my trap."

"You can't trap justice. It's an idea, a belief," Metro Man shot back.

"Well, even the most heartfelt belief can be corroded over time," Megamind told him.

Metro Man would not be shut down. "Justice is a non-corrosive metal," he insisted.

"But metals can be melted by the heat of rev-ange," Megamind said.

"It's *revenge*," Metro Man corrected. "And it's best served cold."

"But it can be easily reheated in the microwave of evil," Megamind reasoned.

Metro Man scoffed. "Well, I think your warranty is about to expire."

"Maybe I got an extended warranty," Megamind countered.

"Warranties are invalid if you don't use the product for its intended purpose," Metro Man replied.

Roxanne had had enough of this silly banter. "Ugh, girls, girls, you're both pretty. Can I go home now?" she asked.

"Of course!" Megamind told her. "That is, if Metro Man can withstand the fully concentrated power of the sun. Fire!" he ordered Minion.

Megamind held his breath, waiting for impact. But nothing happened.

"Minion, fire," he repeated under his breath.

"Uh, it's still warming up," Minion said.

Megamind was outraged. "Warming up? The *sun* is warming up?"

"One second more and just, tippy-tappy-tippy-tap-tap," Minion went on, trying to waste time.

"We are ready in just a few . . . hang on one second," he continued to stall.

"On my way, Roxie," Metro Man said into the screen.

The weapon was still not ready, and Megamind and Minion continued to argue. In fact they were so busy bickering that they did not notice that Metro Man was having trouble flying out of the observatory. Each time he tried to lift himself into the air, he crashed back down to the ground.

Frustrated that his weapon was not working, Megamind dropped his face into his hands. "My spider bite is acting up!" he complained.

"Your plan is failing, just admit it," Roxanne said.

"This is merely the prelude to my real plan," Megamind said, trying to cover. And with that, he took off for the door.

"Same time next week?" Roxanne asked.

Minion waved a can of the knockout spray in front

of her face. Just then, Metro Man slammed into the ceiling again.

"Fargon, dag, crab nuggets!" the hero muttered.

Hearing this, Megamind froze in his tracks. "What did he just say?"

"Crab nuggets?" Minion said.

"Tugtoe, cardpapple, ratflap." Metro Man continued to mutter his nonsense.

Metro Man knew he was trapped—and so did everyone in Metro City who was watching his struggle as it was broadcast on the museum walls.

But Megamind was confused. This was not part of his plan. His plan was to blast Metro Man with his solar-powered rays. His plan certainly was not *this*. Why couldn't Metro Man fly?

"You mad genius, your dark gift has finally paid off," Metro Man told Megamind.

"It . . . it has?" Megamind said, confused.

"This dome is obviously lined with copper, and copper drains my powers," Metro Man struggled to say.

Megamind was astounded. "Your weakness is copper? You're kidding, right?"

But before Metro Man had a chance to answer, the satellite fired a giant beam of light. *Boom!* The bright light blasted through the observatory in an enormous explosion. It was a devastating blast, indeed.

"I don't think even *he* could survive that," Minion said, looking at the wreckage on the computer screen.

"Well, let's not get our hopes up just yet," Megamind said.

Just then, Minion spotted something flying outside the window. "Look!" he shouted.

"Metro Man!" Roxanne shouted, her hopes high.

Megamind looked outside. Sure enough, there was Metro Man—his cape flying behind him in the wind. He flew through the window and crashed on top of Megamind. Only it wasn't *really* Metro Man, it was all that was left of him—a burned skeleton wearing a singed cape.

Yuck!

Megamind tossed the skeleton off of himself.

Roxanne Ritchi gasped.

Minion stared in shock.

"You . . . you did it, sir," Minion stammered.

"I did it?" Megamind said, still not believing what had happened.

Back at the Metro Man Museum, the crowd stared at the projection in stunned disbelief.

"He did it," the mayor said.

Inside the Metro City Penitentiary, the guards and prisoners stared at the television set in stunned disbelief, too.

"He did it," the warden said.

And back at the fake observatory, reality finally hit Megamind.

"I did it!" he shouted. "Metrocity is *mine!*"

CHAPTER FOUR

Megamind and Minion marched toward City Hall, a small army of Brainbots behind them.

"I did it!" Megamind repeated for the millionth time.

"We both did it!" Minion said, wanting some credit for the victory. Then after reconsidering what he said, added, "You, a little bit more than me."

"I, a lot more than you," Megamind boasted.

"But still, when they are giving out the awards, I'm gonna be right there next to you," Minion said.

"What awards? What award ceremony?" Megamind said. "For what? I've dreamed of this moment all my life, Minion."

"So what's the plan, sir?"

"I have no idea." Megamind shrugged. "Hit it!"

And with that, Minion pulled out a boom box and

started to blast music. Megamind danced down the street.

Overhead, helicopters swept the sky. Police in riot gear barricaded the streets, guns drawn.

Suddenly, a huge plume of smoke erupted and surrounded the police. And out of the smoke, dozens of Brainbots emerged, shining their headlights. Terrified, the police lowered their weapons.

Following the Brainbots' entrance, Megamind and Minion appeared, and strutted up the front steps of City Hall. The news cameras captured their every move.

Megamind picked up a microphone and addressed the crowd. "First off, what a turnout! How wild is this, huh? All I did was eliminate the most powerful man in the universe." He let out a chuckle.

"Are there any questions?" Megamind asked the reporters. "Yes, you in the back," he said, pointing to a woman.

Roxanne Ritchi stepped forward. "I'm sure we'd all like to know what you plan to do with us and this city," she said.

"My plan? My plan?" Megamind repeated. "Truth be told, I haven't quite decided what your fate shall be. In the meantime, I want you to carry on with the dreary, normal things you normal people do. Let's just have fun with this! And I will get back to you."

Shielding his face with his cape, Megamind scuttled backward into City Hall and ducked behind the door. Minion scurried in after him.

"Now slam the door really hard," Megamind whispered.

Minion slammed the door, leaving the stunned crowd outside. Megamind cracked up and jumped into Minion's arms.

Minion carried his boss to the mayor's office. (Or what used to be the mayor's office.)

"There he is, Mr. Evil Overlord!" Minion sang.

Megamind jumped out of Minion's arms. "Minion, did you think this day would ever come?"

"No way. Not at all, sir. Never. Never in a million years."

Megamind shot Minion an evil glare.

"I mean, yes. I did," Minion corrected.

Megamind looked around the fancy office. "It's mine, it's all mine! The ceiling fixtures! Look at the intricate moldings. And what's this?" He walked over to the large picture window.

"It's like one of the giant monitors in the lair, but it seems to only carry one station," Megamind remarked.

"It's called a *window*, sir," Minion explained. "You use it to look outside."

Megamind's eyes clouded over. "A window? I've never had a view before," he said, recalling all the years he was locked up.

He gazed at the Metro City skyline. "Metrocity, Minion. It's all mine. If my parents could see me now! And now that Mr. Goody-Two-Shoes is out of the way," he continued, "I can have everything I want!"

And that is exactly what Megamind did. He robbed the banks of all their money, took all the art from the museum, and scared all the citizens from the streets of Metro City.

"Well, this is certainly easy, sir," Minion said, observing the riches piling up in the office. "Everything you always wanted."

Megamind did not look up from his desk. He was busy playing with a toy drinking bird. "Always thirsty, never satisfied. I understand you, little, well-dressed bird. Purposeless. Emptiness. It's a vacuum, isn't it?" He heaved a loud sigh and slumped back in his chair.

"Is something wrong, sir?" Minion asked.

"Just think about it. We have it all, yet we have nothing. It's just too easy now," Megamind said.

"I'm sorry, sir. You've lost me."

"I mean, we did it, right? Then why do I feel so melan-choly?" Megamind asked.

"Melan-choly?" Minion was confused.

"Unhappy," Megamind explained.

"Well, what if tomorrow we kidnap Roxanne Ritchi? That always lifts your spirits," Minion suggested.

Megamind walked over to the window and considered Minion's idea. In the distance he saw the Metro Man statue.

"Good idea," he finally said. "But without him, what's the point?"

"Him?" Minion asked.

"Nothing," Megamind said, not wanting to explain that without a rival in the picture, life was *boring*!

CHAPTER FIVE

"Perhaps we took him for granted, you know? Maybe we never really know how good we have it until it's gone. We miss you, Metro Man. I miss you. And I have just one question for Megamind: Are you happy now? This is Roxanne Ritchi reporting from a city without a hero."

Megamind flipped off the TV and went over to the window. Staring out at the museum, he silently answered Roxanne's question: *No.*

Roxanne finished her broadcast and started to walk up the steps of the museum.

"Wait, Roxie," Hal called after her. "I'm having a party at my house. It's going to be, like, off the hook, or whatever. You should come over. I got a DJ, rented a bouncy house, made a gallon of dip. It's gonna be sick."

"Oh, I don't know, Hal. I don't really feel like being

around a bunch of people," Roxanne said.

"No, no, that's the best part," Hal said. "It'll be, like, you and me."

Roxanne stared at the cameraman. "Wow, that, um, that's certainly very tempting, but—"

"I did hire a wedding photographer," Hal interrupted. "That's just in case something crazy happened and we wanted a picture of it, like maybe we should have this memory, you know?" he rambled.

"I'm going to pass," Roxanne told him. "I have some work here that I need to do."

"Cool. So, Thursday?" Hal asked, not giving up. "Soft Thursday?"

"Good night, Hal," Roxanne said.

"It's a soft *yes* on Thursday," Hal said watching Roxanne walk away. "What's wrong with me?" he said out loud, kicking the news van. "Why don't you love me?"

Roxanne ignored Hal and walked up the steps of the museum. She walked inside. The museum was deserted. She took the elevator up to the top floor, and looked out at the giant statue of Metro Man that stood in the middle of the museum. She was happy to be alone.

Only she wasn't alone.

On the opposite side of the museum, Megamind

took the elevator up to the top floor, too. He stood on the opposite side of the Metro Man statue, a bouquet of flowers in his hand.

"I was in the neighborhood. Thought I'd stop by," Megamind said to the statue. "I've made a horrible mistake. I didn't mean to destroy you. I mean, I *meant* to destroy you, but I didn't think it would really work."

On the other side of the statue, Roxanne Ritchi spoke to the statue, too. "What are we supposed to do? Without you, evil is running rampant through the streets."

"I'm so tired of running rampant through the streets," Megamind said. "What's the point of being bad when there's no good to try to stop you?"

"Someone has to stop Megamind," Roxanne said.

"Hey, we're closing soon," Roxanne heard someone say. Startled, she turned around and saw a man pushing a cart of books.

"Oh, you scared me. Barry, right?" Roxanne asked a soft-spoken man wearing glasses and a sport coat.

"Bernard," the man answered.

"Bernard. I was just, well, I was just talking to myself. You probably think I'm a little bit nuts," Roxanne said.

"I'm not allowed to insult guests directly," Bernard told her.

"Thank you, Bernard. I'll just be another minute."

Bernard shrugged and continued pushing his cart.

Meanwhile, Megamind continued the conversation on his side of the statue. "I had so many evil plans in the works: The Illiteracy Beam, Typhoon Cheese, Robo-Sheep. There are so many battles we will now never have. You know, we never had the chance to say good-bye, so it's good that we have this time now. You know, before I destroy the place."

Megamind reached into the bouquet of flowers he was carrying and set a timer for three minutes and twelve seconds. The flowers were actually a detonator for a bomb!

"Nothing personal," he told the statue, "it just brings back too many painful memories."

Megamind dropped the detonator/bouquet off the balcony. Down below, at the foot of the statue, a Brainbot caught the flowers. Dozens of other Brainbots were stacking dynamite around the statue.

Just then, Megamind heard someone say, "Hello?" and spotted Roxanne Ritchi walking toward him. Frantically, he called out her name. Racing after her, he bumped into Bernard.

"Oh, no," Bernard said. "That's a pretty tasteless costume."

Megamind stopped in his tracks. "Costume?" he asked.

"Megamind's head is not that grossly exaggerated," Bernard said, not realizing that Megamind was actually Megamind.

Megamind quickly scanned Bernard with his watch and then pulled out a futuristic-looking gun.

"Oh, and you even made a cheap replica of his Dehydration Gun. How wonder—"

But before Bernard could finish his sentence, Megamind pointed the gun at him and reduced him to a small, glowing cube.

Seeing a strange flash of light, Roxanne called out, wondering if someone was there.

Instantly, Megamind turned into Bernard, grabbing the man's ID and cell phone.

"Hello, who's there?" Roxanne called out as she ran toward Megamind.

As she rounded a corner, she spotted Bernard (who was really Megamind) pushing his cart.

"Oh, it's just you, Bernard," she said, relieved.

"Oh yes," Megamind answered. "It's just me, *Bernard*."

"Well, thank you for letting me stay," Roxanne told him.

"Look, I wouldn't stay for more than two minutes and thirty-seven seconds," Megamind said, frantically pushing the elevator button. "We're having the walls and ceiling removed."

"Wow, that sounds like quite the renovation. I guess I'll catch a ride down with you," Roxanne said.

Roxanne and Megamind got into the elevator. They rode down in silence, each staring at the Metro Man statue.

Roxanne spoke. "I kept thinking he would do one of his last-minute escapes."

"Yeah, he was really good at those," Megamind said.

"If only the world had a reset button," Roxanne wished.

Megamind's eyes began to tear. "I've looked into the reset button. The science is impossible."

Roxanne looked at Megamind. She was surprised at how emotional he was. Of course, she thought that Megamind was Bernard. "I didn't know you had feelings," she said. "Are you okay?"

Megamind sniffled. "Metro Man's gone. Now there's no one left to challenge Megamind."

"Oh, come on, Bernard. As long as there's evil, good will rise up against it."

That's exactly what Megamind wanted—another hero to fight against.

"I believe someone is going to stand up to Megamind," Roxanne concluded.

Megamind was hopeful. "You really think so?"

Roxanne nodded. "Yeah, it's like they say, heroes aren't born, they're made."

A lightbulb went off in Megamind's head. That was it! Heroes *could* be made. All that was needed were the right ingredients: bravery, strength, determination, and a bit of DNA! It was a brilliant plan, indeed. Laughing, Megamind scooped up Roxanne and twirled her around. Suddenly, he stopped.

"I think we should run," Megamind said, remembering the bomb that was set to go off.

The two raced outside, and Megamind put Roxanne safely into a cab. Once she was gone, he turned back into his villainous self.

"Time to put the past behind us," Megamind said out loud. "Only the future matters."

And with that, the museum exploded, sending Megamind flying through the air.

CHAPTER SIX

The next morning, Megamind stood in his secret hideout, his villainous spirit renewed. He had just filled Minion in on his plan.

"Create a hero! Wait, what?" Minion was confused. He just stood there, staring at Megamind and holding an open box of doughnuts. "Why would you do that?" Minion finally managed to say.

"So I have someone to fight. Minion, I'm a villain without a hero. A yin with no yang. A bullfighter with no bull to fight. In other words, I'm bored!" Megamind explained, taking the doughnuts from Minion and throwing them in the air.

"Now, ask me how I'm going to do it," Megamind prodded. "Go on, ask."

Minion obeyed. "How are you gonna do it?"

Megamind climbed over Minion and jumped onto a rolling library ladder. He showed Minion the wall chart he had created, and pointed to items on it as he spoke.

"I'm going to give someone, I don't know who yet, Metro Man's powers. I'm going to train that someone to become Metrocity's new hero. After that, I'm going to debut this said hero so he will win the hearts and minds of the people."

Megamind pulled a sheet off of a painting and revealed his last step. "Then finally, I'm going to fight that hero in an epic battle of good and evil, which will put everything back the way it was when it was perfect and rosy."

"How are you going to give someone superpowers?" Minion asked.

Megamind rushed to a lab desk that was covered with Metro Man's cape. "Behold, Minion! Metro Man's cape! Look closely—tell me what you see."

Minion picked up a magnifying glass and studied the cape. "Dandruff?" he suggested.

"Yes!" Megamind shouted. "It's his DNA. From this, we'll extract the source of Metro Man's awesome power."

Minion understood the plan. Now it was time to get to work. But after putting Metro Man's dandruff into the DNA chamber, he began to have second thoughts. Maybe this wasn't such a good idea after all.

"Sir, I think this is a bad idea," Minion announced.

"Yes, this is a very, wickedly, bad idea for the greater good of bad," Megamind said.

"You might think this idea is good in your bad perception, which makes bad, good," Minion explained, "but from a good perception, it's just plain bad."

"Oh, you don't know what's good for bad," Megamind told him.

Megamind turned back to the DNA machine just as it released a tiny drop of precious liquid into a pellet. Carefully, Megamind picked up the pellet with a pair of tongs and loaded it into his Infuser Gun.

"Now, we have just one shot at this. We must find a suitable subject. Someone of noble heart and mind, who puts the welfare of others above their own," Megamind explained to Minion.

Suddenly, a cell phone rang. "What on earth is that?" a confused Megamind asked.

"It seems to be emanating from there, sir," Minion said, pointing to Megamind's pants.

Megamind reached into his pocket and pulled out Bernard's phone. Clearly, he had never seen one before.

"Um . . . ollo?" he said awkwardly into the phone.

"It's *hello*," Minion whispered.

"Oh. Hello?" Megamind repeated.

"Hey, it's Roxanne," a voice on the other end said. "I just want to thank you for inspiring me the other day."

"Yes . . . you inspired me, too," Megamind replied.

"Great! I think we can find out what Megamind has planned for the city and stop it. I'm already hot on his trail," she said, thinking she was speaking with Bernard. After all, she *did* call Bernard's cell phone; who else would she be speaking to?

"Oh, really?" Megamind said, intrigued. Then he covered up the phone and said to Minion, "She's so cute."

Just then, Minion spotted Roxanne on the security camera. She and Hal, who was carrying a camera, were standing right outside their secret hideout! How in the world did she find them?

"This is the only building in Metro City with a fake observatory on the roof," Roxanne said, explaining how she discovered them.

Megamind was shocked. But then again, there was no way they'd find the secret entrance. He and Minion were safe as long as they remained inside.

Suddenly Roxanne gasped. "Look, Hal," she said.

"There's a doormat here that says *Secret Entrance*." She pushed her hand against the wall and walked through.

Megamind shot Minion a look. *"Minion!"* he shouted.

Minion shrugged. "I kept forgetting where it was!"

"She'll discover all our secrets! You dim-witted creation of science!" Megamind exclaimed, pushing Minion into a storage cabinet.

"What?" Megamind heard Roxanne say over the phone.

"What? Oh no, not you, Roxanne," he said, trying to recover. "I was just yelling at my . . . mother's urn. Don't do anything, I'll be right there."

Megamind quickly pulled a curtain over the wall chart that outlined all his plans and turned himself into Bernard.

Roxanne continued to explore, leaving poor Hal behind outside.

"Roxanne?" Hal called out. "Oh no. Not again! I was supposed to protect her."

Roxanne walked farther into Megamind's hideout. Suddenly, she heard someone call out her name. She spun around to find Bernard (who was really Megamind in disguise) standing there.

"I'm glad you're here," a relieved Roxanne said. Then

she stopped. "Wait, how did you get here so fast?

"Well, I . . . I happened to be speed-walking nearby when you called," Megamind said.

"In a suit?" Roxanne asked, looking Megamind up and down.

Uh-oh, what was he going to think of now? "It's called formal speed-walking," Megamind said quickly. "But that's not important. I better take the lead. This way looks exciting," he said, trying to steer her toward an Exit sign.

"It says *Exit*," Roxanne told him.

"Which is the abbreviation for *exciting*, right?" Megamind said with a smile.

Just then, Roxanne spotted a curtain and whipped it open to reveal Megamind's wall chart.

Roxanne let out a low whistle. "I think we just hit the mother lode."

Megamind shook his head. "It was probably left by the previous tenant."

"No, this is Megamind's," Roxanne said, ripping off a little piece of paper. "The jelly's still wet. Just look at this thing!"

Without looking, Roxanne handed the paper to Megamind. He immediately stuffed it in his mouth.

"With your expertise on all things Megamind and my nosy reporter skills, we can find out what that villain has planned for this city and stop it!" Roxanne announced.

"Oh, what fun!" Megamind told Roxanne.

When Roxanne turned her back for a moment, Megamind frantically whispered into his wrist communicator. "Minion, Code: Send in the Brainbots!"

Inside the storage closet, Minion was studying an instruction manual. "You know, the whole point of a code is—"

"Oh, Code: Do it, Minion," Megamind cut him off.

Minion obeyed, and pressed a button. Suddenly, a squad of Brainbots crashed through the wall behind Roxanne. But instead of grabbing the reporter, they grabbed Megamind. (They thought he was Bernard, after all.)

"What are you doing?" Megamind cried out. "Let me go! Let me go!"

"Bernard!" Roxanne cried out in fear as she saw him being dragged away by the mechanical monsters.

The Brainbots flew Megamind around a corner, knocking over the storage closet with Minion inside. The closet door opened, and the Infuser Gun tumbled out. Seeing the gun, Roxanne picked it up.

Out of Roxanne's sight, Megamind turned off his disguise. "It's me, you fools," he told the Brainbots.

Immediately, the robots dropped him, and he crashed in a heap on the floor.

"Megamind!" he heard Roxanne call out. "What have you done with Bernard?"

"Oh, Bernard? Oh yes, I'm doing horrible things to that man," Megamind said from his hiding place. "I don't want to get into it, but lasers, spikes—"

"Oh, please no, not the lasers and the spikes," Megamind said in Bernard's voice.

"You know the drill," Megamind said.

And switching back to Bernard, he responded, "Oh no, not the drill! *Aaaaah!*"

"Let him go, or . . . ," Roxanne started.

"Or what?" Megamind said.

"Or I'm going to find out what this weird-looking gun does," she said, pointing the Infuser Gun at him.

Panicked, Megamind said, "Don't shoot! I mean, I'll just go get him."

Megamind threw open a door to a crawl space and dived inside.

"Unhand me, you fiend!" Bernard's voice called, popping his head out of the crawl space.

"His strength . . . It's too much," a strained Bernard said.

Megamind popped his head out. "I work out," he said.

"Well, it's really paying off," Bernard said. "You're so fit and strangely charismatic."

Finally, Megamind (as Bernard) stumbled out of the crawl space and collapsed against a wall.

"Are you okay?" Roxanne asked, rushing to his side.

"I did my best," Megamind/Bernard told her. "But he's too fantastic. Here, let me carry that heavy gun."

Megamind tried to take the gun from Roxanne, but she refused. She was in charge of this operation. Roxanne walked around a corner. Behind her, Megamind growled in frustration and turned back into himself.

"Let go, it's mine," he said, jumping in front of Roxanne and trying to grab the gun.

They fell to the floor, wrestling for the weapon.

"You're going to break it," Megamind told her.

"Give it to me!" Roxanne yelled.

Suddenly, the gun fired. The pellet bounced off the wall and flew into a pipe. The pellet was gone—and so was Megamind's only chance to create a new hero! Or was it?

On the security monitor, Megamind spotted Hal, who was waiting for Roxanne. "Roxanne?" Hal called out. He poked his head in front of an exposed pipe and— *Bam!* Something smacked into him and knocked him flat on the ground. Hal had been hit by Megamind's DNA pellet!

Meanwhile, Roxanne was still trying to flee Megamind and find Bernard. Where had the villain hidden her friend? She opened a door and raced straight toward an alligator pit. Desperately, she tried to slow down to stop from falling into the pit. Just then, a pair of arms grabbed her from behind.

"Bernard!" she exclaimed, looking back at her hero. "You were right about that door being exciting."

Megamind knew they had no time for idle chatter. The Brainbots were hot on their trail. They turned and raced down the hall.

As they ran, Roxanne spotted a stick of dynamite, grabbed it, and, using a Brainbot, lit it.

"What are you doing?" Megamind asked.

"This will stop them. Here," she said, throwing the stick of dynamite to him.

Frantically, Megamind tried to blow out the fuse.

"Just throw it!" Roxanne shouted.

As he tossed the stick, Megamind whispered, "Daddy's sorry."

Mistaking the dynamite for a game of fetch, a Brainbot tried to bring the stick back to Megamind.

"Ahh! Stay!" Megamind shouted, seeing the Brainbot flying behind him.

But the Brainbot didn't have time to obey Megamind's command. For in the next instant, the dynamite exploded, sending Megamind and Roxanne flying through the air and out the front door!

CHAPTER SEVEN

Megamind and Roxanne landed on the ground outside Megamind's hideout.

"Wow, that was exciting! You were very strong in there," Roxanne told Megamind, thinking he was Bernard.

"I know," Megamind agreed.

"I've never seen anyone but Metro Man stand up to him like that," Roxanne commented.

"I just did what a very slim minority of people would do in such a situation," Megamind told her.

Just then, Hal popped up from the ground below them. "What's going on?" he asked.

"Hal, what happened?" a surprised Roxanne asked.

"I think a bee flew up my nose," Hal told her. "I was just about to make my frontal assault to rescue you, but, like, fifty ninjas tried to attack me so I had to beat 'em all up, and I did, and they were all, like, crying and stuff," he exaggerated.

Two could play at the exaggeration game. "Wow, a brave one, isn't he?" Megamind said.

"Who are you?" Hal asked.

"Oh, this is Bernard," Roxanne explained. "He's my partner.

Hal was confused. What did Roxanne mean by *partner*? *He* was her partner, not this old guy. Who did he think he was?

Roxanne looked at Hal and then back at Bernard. "Look, I better take him home," she said, pointing at Hal. "Do you need a ride home?"

Seeing an out, Megamind said, "Perhaps we should split up just in case Megamind tries to follow us."

"Smart thinking," Roxanne said, throwing her arm around him. "I'll call you tomorrow, partner!"

"Yeah, okay," a confused Megamind said. "I'd like that."

"That was weird for everybody," Hal said as he and Roxanne walked toward the van. "You accidentally hugged him instead of me."

Roxanne shook her head and took her cameraman home. He certainly needed to rest!

Megamind watched the pair leave, a silly smile on his lips. Suddenly, Minion's voice came blaring through his wrist communicator.

"Sir?" Minion called. "Did you find out who it was?"

Megamind snapped out of his trance and whispered into his communicator. "Code: Get the car!"

"Code: Right away, sir," Minion responded.

A few minutes later, Minion pulled up in the invisible car and Megamind hopped in.

Megamind asked Minion to fill him in on the details about Hal, the man they'd infused with godlike powers.

"Well, sir, his name's Hal Stewart. He's twenty-eight years old. No criminal record. Actually, no records at all. Apparently this man hasn't accomplished anything," Minion reported.

"Not yet, Minion. Not yet," Megamind said, thinking about how Hal would change.

But Minion was convinced they had made a mistake. Hal was not the hero they were looking for. He took out the Infuser Gun and set it to "defuse." One blast of the thing, and Hal would be back to normal. Megamind, however, had another plan. In fact, his plan was already in motion.

"This is no mistake," he told Minion. "It's destiny."

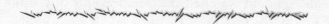

Megamind and Minion arrived at Hal's apartment, and blasted through the door. The blast was so strong that it collapsed Hal's Murphy bed back into the wall—with Hal still in it!

"Hal Shtewart," Megamind announced. "Prepare for your destiny! Hal? Hal Shtewart? Am I saying it right?"

"Stewart," Minion corrected.

Megamind and Minion looked around the room. It was empty. Then they heard a muffled voice coming from the bed in the wall. Minion pulled down the bed.

"Is this a robbery?" a terrified Hal asked. "Because the lady across the hall has way better stuff than me."

"Ooh, look, it's Hal Stewart," Megamind said to Minion. "Quick, the spray."

Minion pulled out the knockout spray, but the can was empty. He had probably used it one too many times on Roxanne Ritchi. Quickly, Minion whipped out his Forget-Me-Stick and knocked Hal over the head. The guy was out cold.

Minion and Megamind stared at Hal. Minion was still not convinced that the guy would make a good hero. But Megamind was sure he could craft a hero out of him.

He pushed Hal and his bed back up into the wall, and looked around the apartment.

"A potter couldn't ask for finer clay," he said. "I smell a hero!"

"I smell something burning," Minion said.

Megamind looked behind the bed and saw something glowing. "I think it's working. Places! Places! Do you have your disguise?" he asked Minion.

Megamind pressed a button on his watch and was instantly transformed into a gray-haired old man in a spandex suit. He was Space Dad—the perfect disguise, indeed!

Minion reached into his pack and pulled out a curly wig and a *Kiss the Cook* apron.

Just then, two muscular arms burst out from behind the bed. The bed fell down and out popped the new, superpowered version of Hal Stewart.

"Rise, my glorious creation. Rise, and come to Papa!" Megamind said.

"What's going on?" a confused Hal asked.

"I sent you to this planet to teach you about justice, honor, and nobility," Megamind told him. "I am your father."

"So you're like my Space Dad?" Hal asked.

"Yeah, I'm like your Space Dad," Megamind said, patting his gray hair.

Turning to Minion, Hal asked, "And you are what?"

"I'm your Space Stepmom," Minion responded. "I've had some work done recently."

"Is this some kind of dream?" Hal asked.

Megamind went on to tell Hal that he had been blessed with unfathomable power and that they were there to guide him on the path to becoming Metro City's new hero. And in that role, he would battle the supergenius of Megamind.

Minion held up a mirror so Hal could see his new look. Then, Megamind held up a photo of Metro Man flying with Roxanne Ritchi in his arms. Only it wasn't exactly Metro Man—the image of Hal's head was on Metro Man's shoulders!

"I know this is a lot to take in," Megamind told Hal. "It may take months for you to come to grips with—"

"No way," Hall interrupted. And with that, he backflipped straight through the wall.

"Wait! I wasn't finished!" Megamind called after him.

Megamind ran to the hole in the wall, looked out, and surveyed the situation. Down below, he saw a bunch of cars piled in a heap. Apparently, Hal's appearance had startled the drivers and created an accident. As Megamind scanned the scene for Hal, he saw the new hero burst out of the pileup and sprint down the street cheering.

"*Waa-hooo!* I'm gonna be a hero," Hal called out.

Then he scaled the side of a skyscraper and jumped up and down, shaking his fists in the air.

"*Waa-hooo!* I'm gonna be a hero!" he repeated. "I'm gonna be a hero!"

"See, Minion," Megamind said as he watched Hal's antics from the wall of the apartment. "He's perfect!"

Megamind was pleased—he had created the ultimate hero!

CHAPTER EIGHT

Megamind had succeeded in the creation part, but now he needed to *teach* Hal how to be the perfect hero. Megamind went to his idea chart on the wall and circled the word *mentor*. Step two of his plan was about to begin.

Megamind and Minion (who were still in their disguises) wrangled Hal and brought him to Megamind's warehouse. It was time to practice being a hero.

A stage was set up to look like a bank robbery was in progress, and Minion was tied up as a hostage. Hal burst onto the stage, grabbed the Megamind dummy, and started punching it in the head.

"Stop!" Megamind called from the sidelines.

"What?" Hal wanted to know what he had done wrong.

"My son, when you're fighting Megamind, you take

him to jail. Metro Man always valued life and preserved it at all costs," Megamind said, offering some fatherly advice.

"Seems like an extra step to me," Hal said.

Megamind knew he had to keep on training Hal if he wanted to turn him into the perfect hero. He took Hal outside to practice flying. He attached Hal to a rope, handed the rope to Minion, and raised Hal into the sky like a kite.

"No! No! Arms up, stomach down! Like Metro Man!" Megamind shouted to his student as he tugged on the string.

"Metro Man! Metro Man! If Metro Man's so cool, why don't you go be his Space Dad?" Hal complained.

And with that, he took off flying, dragging Minion behind him on the rope.

Even though Hal wasn't the best student, Megamind and Minion did not give up.

Megamind wanted Hal to practice facing off with Megamind. Since the real Megamind was still in his Space Dad disguise, he did the next best thing—he created a Megamind mask.

Megamind put on the mask and, using his real voice, said, "The flames of my evil burn bright."

He pulled up his mask. "Now you say something cool back to me," he said.

"I don't know . . . I'm feeling like you're not giving me anything," Hal said.

"I'm giving you gold!" an outraged Megamind responded. "Metro Man would hit that back with a top spin!"

"I feel like I need a little superhero break," Hal said. "You keep working, though."

And with that, Hal exited through the wall. Megamind threw up his hands in exasperation.

"I don't know what to do with this kid!"

"Well, he doesn't get it from my side," Minion joked.

Just then, Megamind's phone rang. He looked down and saw that he had a text message from Roxanne. It read: *Meet me at library, partner . . . RR.*

"Can't wait," Megamind said as he typed back a message.

"Can't wait for what?" Minion asked.

"It's that foul minx Roxanne Ritchi," Megamind said, trying to make Minion think that he didn't care about her. "She's determined to figure out our secret plan and report it to the whole city."

"Oh no," a concerned Minion responded.

"So I must throw her off our trail," Megamind concluded. And with that he turned to leave.

"That sounds risky," Minion warned.

"No! But I must, Minion," Megamind said with dramatic flair. "As distasteful and unpleasant as the experience will surely be, I must!"

Megamind turned on his Bernard disguise and went to the library to meet Roxanne.

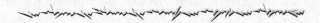

Megamind and Roxanne were having a wonderful time together, laughing and exchanging stories.

"Bernard, I never knew you were so funny," Roxanne said.

"And I never heard you laugh before," Megamind told her.

"Yeah, it's been a while," Roxanne admitted. "Feels pretty good."

Megamind picked up a book and flipped to a page that had a picture of Metro Man, looking extremely cool, hauling Megamind off to jail.

"He had it all, didn't he?" Megamind said, looking at the book. "The powers. Cool hair. No wonder all the ladies swooned over him."

Roxanne shook her head. "I wouldn't say *all* the ladies swooned. Personally, he's not really my type."

"But I thought you two were . . . ," Megamind began.

"Everyone did," Roxanne cut in. "You know, the hero and the reporter? But no, I prefer more brain than brawn," she said before opening a book.

Megamind hid his smile. "You don't say."

After they were done selecting their library books—hers were on genetics and physics, his were on parenting and rearing teens—Megamind walked Roxanne home.

Megamind was lost in thought. "Something bothering you, Bernard?" Roxanne asked, wondering why her friend had grown so quiet.

"Actually, I'm sort of mentoring this troubled youth," Megamind began.

Roxanne was impressed. "Wow, Bernard, that's really sweet."

"I can't seem to get through to him to realize his full potential. Do you know anybody like that?" Megamind asked.

Roxanne laughed. "Oh yeah, there's Hal."

Megamind's ears perked up. "Yes! Tell me about Hal."

"Hal is inherently lazy, unmotivated, and immature," Roxanne listed.

"How did you dominate and control him?" Megamind wanted to know.

"I gave him a little encouragement," Roxanne answered.

"Is that available over-the-counter?" Megamind asked.

Roxanne smiled. "Positive feedback. I just said, 'Hal, you're special and I appreciate your contribution.'"

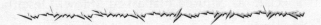

Later that day, when it was time to tutor Hal, Megamind decided to try Roxanne's approach. He watched Minion struggle with the rope as Hal flew in the air. Hal was up in the air all right, but he was holding a giant locomotive up there with him!

"Put that down!" Minion scolded him.

"You can't tell me what to do Space Stepmom," Hal said. "Look at the word between *space* and *mom*. *Step*. So step back."

"Great progress, Hal," Megamind put in.

Minion was surprised at Megamind's praise. "What? He's defiant! He's rude!"

"He's expressing himself. I think that's wonderful," Megamind said with a proud smile.

Hal flew down. "C'mon, Space Dad. When do I get my costume? I'm ready. Space Stepmom won't let me do anything."

Suddenly, Megamind punched Hal in the stomach. Hal doubled over, and Megamind jumped on his back.

"Let's go for a ride," Megamind commanded.

"Hal, I think you're special," Megamind told his as they flew. "And I appreciate your contribution."

"Special?" a confused Hal asked. "How? Describe it. Go into detail."

"You will be the beloved hero of the entire city," Megamind told him. "A symbol of what we all aspire to be. People will love you."

"Even chicks?" Hal asked.

"Especially chicks. And all other farm animals. I've seen it firsthand," Megamind said.

"Well, what're we waiting for? We've got training to do!" Hal exclaimed.

The pair headed toward the high school gym. Megamind put on his Megamind mask and once again faced off with Hal.

"The flames of my evil burn bright," Megamind declared.

"Well, the fires of evil can be blown out by the cold winds of righteousness," Hal responded.

"Wind is like a promise," Megamind said. "Easily broken."

"But a broken promise can be mended with the Scotch Tape of Horror," Hal said back.

"Scotch tape is one-sided, while evil is sticky on both," Megamind told him.

"The water of nobility will wash away the sticky," Hal responded.

Okay, that was it—Megamind did not know what to say. Hal had actually done a good job at banter. Still, he wanted to encourage his student. So he whipped off his mask and said, "Not bad, my son." What else was there to say?

Soon all the lessons and encouragement began to take effect. Hal learned to fly and Megamind was able to let go of the rope.

"Be free, my beautiful dove," Megamind said as Hal soared through the air. Then he turned to Minion and said, "Minion, I think you're special. And I appreciate your contribution."

Minion was touched. "Thank you! Thank you so much!"

Megamind smiled. It looked like all his hard work was about to pay off.

CHAPTER NINE

Megamind wanted to share his good news with Roxanne. Well, not *all* of the news—just the part that he had finally broken through to Hal. He went to Roxanne's apartment.

"Thanks for the advice, Roxanne," Megamind (as Bernard) told her. "The kid is actually going to graduate."

"That's wonderful, Bernard. Glad I could help. Hey, why don't we celebrate over dinner. Tomorrow night. Got any plans?"

"Dinner? You mean like a social feeding courtship ritual?" Megamind asked.

Roxanne laughed. "I think people call it a date, Bernard."

Roxanne turned her attention to a piece of paper. They were trying to rebuild Megamind's idea wall.

"So we know he's doing something with genetic code over here. I think that's the key. Once we figure out what it's for, we can expose that little blue twerp's twisted plan."

"How can you judge his plan if you don't even know what it is yet?" Megamind asked. "That seems a little unfair."

Roxanne turned away from the wall to think. And when she did, Megamind quickly switched around some of the pieces on the idea wall!

"Unfair? Bernard, he's evil," Roxanne declared.

"I'm just saying if you really want to take on Megamind, you might want to step back and try to understand him a little better."

"Let me show you what I understand," Roxanne said, dropping a thick file on the table.

Megamind stared at the file. "What's this?"

"Megamind's prison file," she told him.

"Where did you get this?" Megamind wanted to know.

"The prison," Roxanne said.

"Oh, right," Megamind said, feeling a bit embarrassed.

"I was going through it last night and happened on this." Roxanne flipped through the file and pulled out a picture of baby Megamind.

Megamind's heart sank.

"Turns out he actually grew up in that prison," Roxanne said. "Can you believe it?"

Megamind remembered his parents putting him in the spaceship as their planet was being destroyed.

"You are destined for greatness," his father had told him.

Megamind's memory flashed from his trip in that pod to landing at the penitentiary to making license plates there.

Roxanne's voice snapped him out of his daydream. "How did this cute little baby turn out so evil?"

"Maybe he never had a choice," Megamind said. "It was obviously the path of fate."

"Fate?" Roxanne said incredulously. "We choose our path, Bernard. Our path doesn't choose us."

Megamind bit his tongue. He didn't want to argue with Roxanne. But silently he told himself how wrong she was.

Roxanne pulled out a newspaper clipping and showed it to Megamind. "Look at this. When's the last time you threatened to melt a bank? When was the last time you tried to build a laser cannon on a mountaintop.

72

When was the last time you turned the Atlantic Ocean into Jell-O?"

"I'm sure that outcome was completely unintentional," Megamind said sheepishly.

"What I'm saying is, you've chosen to be good."

Megamind was silent. Roxanne was talking to him, but clearly *he* had not chosen to be good. Roxanne didn't know who he really was.

Megamind looked down and saw that Roxanne was holding his hand.

That only made things more complicated.

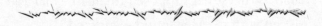

That evening, as the sun was about to set, Megamind brought Hal up to a hill that overlooked the city.

"Do you have somebody special in your life, Hal?" Megamind asked.

"Yeah, me," a cocky Hal answered.

"No. I mean someone you want to love and cherish and keep away from all the hurt," Megamind explained.

"Oh, oh. A babe," Hal said, understanding what Megamind was getting at. "No, not yet. But, there's this really, really good-looking one that I've got my eye on currently."

Megamind nodded. "That's very good. Romance is very inspiring. All you have to do is save her and she'll be yours."

"That's what I hear," Hal said.

"Well, I think you're ready for this," Megamind said, handing Hal a wrapped gift box.

Hal opened the box and saw a tiny red costume with the letter *T* on the front.

"Don't worry, it stretches," Megamind told him.

Hal looked puzzled. "What's the *T* stand for?"

"Titan," Megamind told him.

"Titan? What's that supposed to mean?" Hal asked.

"Just go with it," Megamind instructed.

Finally, it was time for Hal's debut as Titan.

"I'm so proud of you, Hal," Megamind said.

"Honestly, no one's ever said that to me before," Hal admitted.

"Honestly, I've never said that to anyone before," Megamind said.

Just then, Minion walked up to them. "Who wants churros?" he asked, waving the doughnut-like treats.

"I do!" an excited Hal answered.

"I do!" Megamind echoed. "Churros all around!"

"Thanks, Space Stepmom," Hal said.

74

"On the count of three, unsheathe your churro!" Megamind called out. "One, two, three."

They all held up their churros like swords.

"To Titan!" Megamind said. "Tomorrow, the city will know your name."

CHAPTER TEN

The next day, Roxanne and Megamind (as Bernard) were standing with a big crowd in front of the museum. They watched as a new hero flew overhead. Quick as a flash, Titan assembled the scattered pieces of the Metro Man statue and created a new figure. Then he carved a big *T* into its chest.

"Please, tell me you're getting this!" Roxanne said to Megamind, who was holding the camera.

Megamind nodded, and filmed it all.

Reporters crowded around Titan as he landed. Cameras flashed; reporters shouted questions.

"You can rest easy, people. Nothing bad shall ever happen anymore. Because of me. You're welcome," Titan announced.

The reporters wanted more. Who was this guy?

Titan held up his hands. "Whoa, whoa, whoa. Please, one at a time. Let's go by order of hotness. Roxie, you're first."

Roxanne Ritchi was startled. "Do I know you?" she asked Titan.

"No . . . I've just been a big fan of your journalistic reporting of . . . journalistic stuff . . . ," he faltered, trying not to give away his real identity.

Quickly, Megamind stepped up, hoping to help Titan out. "Say, do you happen to have a prepared statement of some kind?" he asked.

"Oh, that reminds me," Titan said. "I have a prepared statement of some kind." He reached into his shorts and pulled out a balled-up piece of paper.

"Villains of Metro City," Titan strained to read the words. "Your time is a hand."

"I think you mean *at* hand," Megamind whispered.

"Yes, thank you, nerd," Titan said, thinking Megamind was really Bernard.

Then he crumpled up the speech and threw it away. "Megamind, I'm calling you out. Meet me at City Hall Plaza. Early. Not too early. Like, after breakfast."

"What's your name?" Roxanne asked.

"Tighten."

And now the citizens of Metro City knew the name of the man who had come to save them.

Later that night, Megamind and Minion watched the news coverage of the day's events.

"Looks like soon the city will be saved and everything back to normal," a reporter said. "All thanks to one man . . ."

Megamind looked at the bottom of the screen. It read: TIGHTEN.

"I guess I should have written down the spelling for him," Megamind said, shaking his head. "Oh well. How long is this going to take?" he asked Minion, who was measuring him for a new suit.

"Just a few alterations, sir, and I will be done with your most terrifying cape yet," Minion told him. "I'm calling it the Black Mamba."

"Oh, gosh!" Megamind cried out suddenly. "I am running late, I have to go."

"What? Where are you going, sir? We have our debut battle with Tighten tomorrow morning. We haven't even tested your big battle suit yet," Minion said.

"You attend to the details, Minion," Megamind told him. "I have to run a few errands."

Minion looked around, confused. Megamind needed to prepare for battle! Just then he sniffed the air.

"Are you wearing cologne?" he asked Megamind.

"No, that's just my natural musk," Megamind lied, covering his armpits. "Now, where are the car keys?"

But as Megamind walked toward the counter, Minion shot out his robotic arm and snapped up the keys.

Now everything was making sense. "This is about Miss Ritchi, isn't it?" Minion asked. "You're going on a date with her!"

Megamind chuckled. "Nooo, my main man! Get out of town!"

"Oh, this is bad. This is bad. You've fallen in love with her!" Minion shouted.

"You are forgetting your place, Minion. Now give me the keys."

Minion extended his arm beyond Megamind's reach.

"What happens when Roxanne finds out who you really are?"

"She will never find out," Megamind said. "That's the point of *lyyying*." And with that, he pressed a button on Minion's robotic chest and Minion's extended arm fell limp. Megamind picked up the keys and walked toward the car.

"No!" Minion shouted, still trying to stop him.

Minion pressed a button on a remote and the invisible car disappeared. Megamind stumbled and dropped the keys.

"This has gone far enough!" Minion shouted, grabbing the keys and dropping them into his fishbowl head.

"That was really grown-up!" Megamind shouted, chasing after Minion.

"Sir, sir, please get a hold of yourself," Minion begged.

"I will flush you," Megamind warned.

"It's for your own good," Minion shouted back.

"What do you know?" Megamind asked.

"I may not know much, but I do know this: The bad guy doesn't get the girl."

"You may be right. You *don't* know much," Megamind said. "Now give me the keys."

Minion pressed the button again. The car reappeared and Megamind smashed right into it.

"My sole purpose in life is to look after you," Minion explained.

"Well, I don't *need* you to look after me," Megamind shot back.

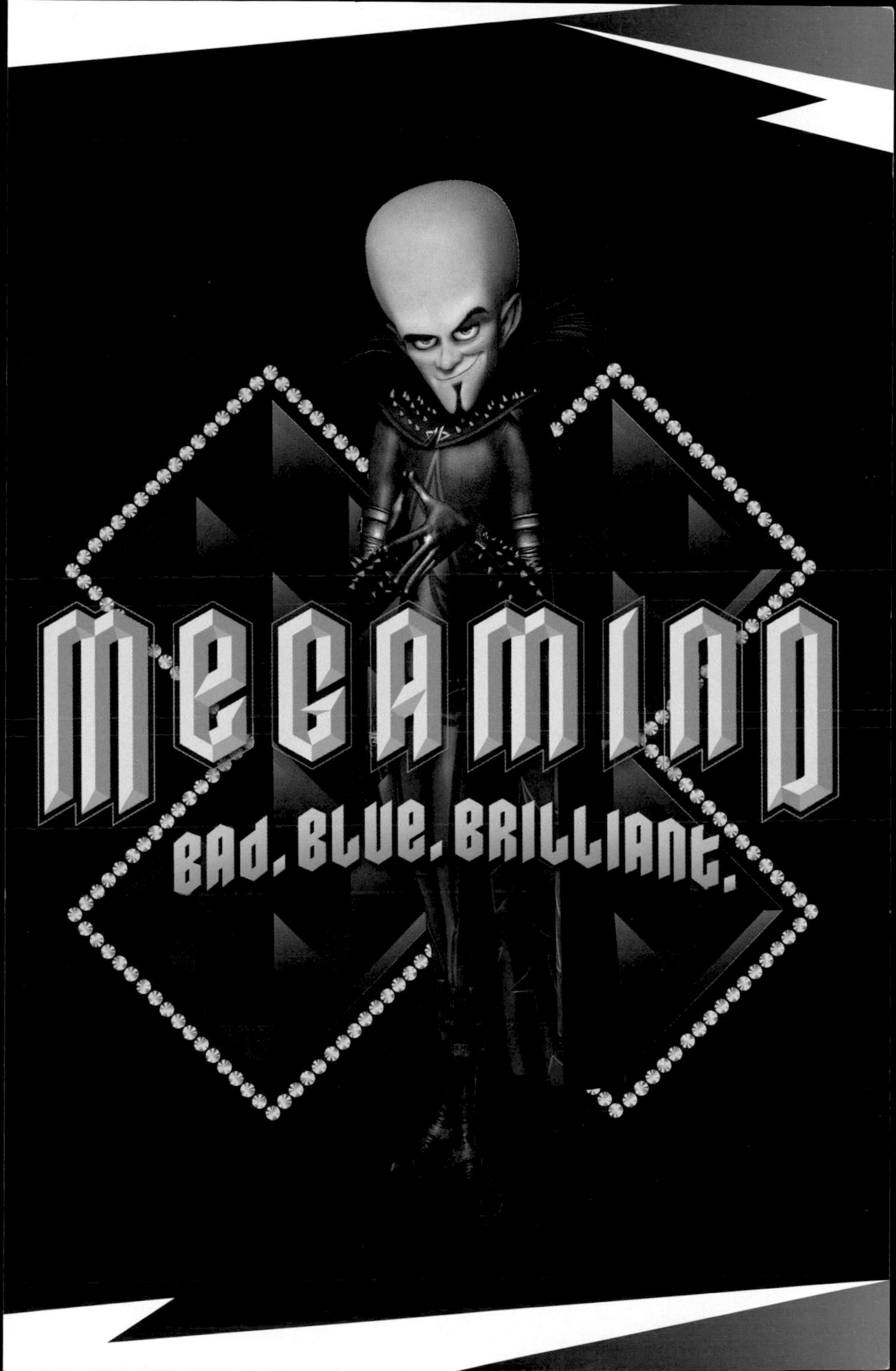
MEGAMIND
BAD. BLUE. BRILLIANT.

Roxanne Ritchi

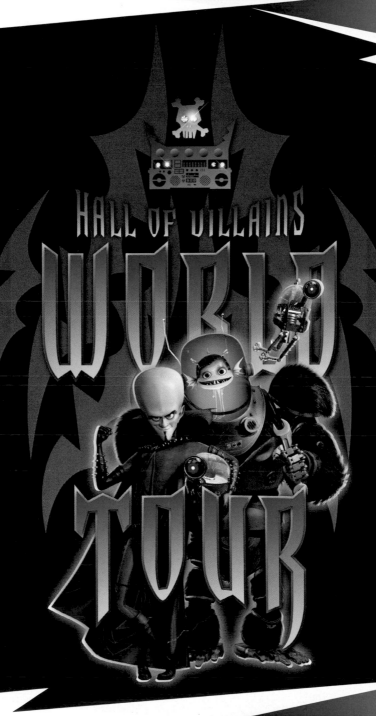

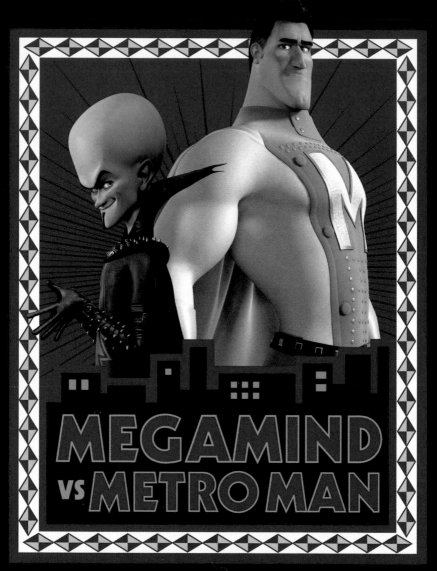

MEGAMIND vs METRO MAN

Minion was shocked. Was Megamind really saying that he didn't need him?

"Let me make it clear," Megamind reinforced. "Code: I Don't Need You."

Minion had had enough. He threw the car keys on the ground and said, "Code: I'll just pack my things and go!"

Sucking back tears, Minion walked away.

Megamind got into the car and stared at himself in the mirror, trying to force a smile. But it was no use— his best friend was gone and he was masquerading as someone else trying to get the girl. Would his plan work, or was Minion right?

Megamind sighed, turned on his Bernard disguise, and forced a smile. It was time for his date.

CHAPTER ELEVEN

Roxanne Ritchi was in her apartment, talking on the phone to her mother. Roxanne was telling her about the most wonderful man she had ever met. A man named Bernard. He was smart and charming (even though he couldn't fly, much to her mother's disappointment). Roxanne finished her conversation with her mother. She needed to get ready for her date with Bernard.

As Roxanne knelt down to put on her shoes, she caught a reflection of the idea wall in the sliding glass door of her balcony. Suddenly, everything came together. Tighten—Megamind had *created* him. Stunned, Roxanne walked out onto her balcony.

"Hey, Roxie!" someone called out.

Roxanne spun around. It was Tighten, and he was floating just off her balcony. Roxanne screamed.

"I usually just scare criminals," Tighten told her. "You haven't been naughty, have you?"

Roxanne laughed nervously.

"I'm totally messing with you. You're funny!" Tighten exclaimed. Then he grabbed her and took off.

"Whoa! What do you think you're doing?" Roxanne asked, alarmed.

"Oh, am I moving too fast?" Tighten asked. "You're probably right. I should just rescue you a few times before we get all romantic. Whoops!"

And with that, he dropped her in midair. Roxanne fell for about twenty feet before Tighten caught her.

"Saved ya!" Tighten shouted. "You are lucky to have such a great hero here."

"Don't you ever . . . ," Roxanne started. Then she punched the "hero" on the chin.

Once again, Tighten dropped her. And once again, Roxanne plummeted to the ground. And, yes, once again, Tighten saved her.

Tighten carried Roxanne in his arms as he flew through traffic. Roxanne was petrified—this guy was totally nuts!

"Building ahead!" Roxanne shouted.

Tighten tossed Roxanne over the building, smashed

through the walls, and caught her on the other side.

"Gotcha!" Tighten called out. "I'm sorry, what were you saying? I couldn't hear you over the sound of me saving your life."

"Put me down, right now!" Roxanne demanded.

"Okay, all right," Tighten relented. "Hold on."

Tighten landed on the roof of Metro City Tower. Finally, he set Roxanne down.

"Are you crazy?!" Roxanne screamed at him.

"I suppose I am a little crazy—about you," Tighten answered as he flew upside down.

Roxanne backed away. "Who are you, really?" She wanted Tighten to admit to her who he actually was.

"Oh, oh, right. Well, prepare to have your mind blown, little lady."

Tighten pulled off his mask.

"Hal?!" Roxanne asked.

"Yeah! Isn't this great? Now there's nothing keeping us apart," Tighten told her.

"No, it's not great," Roxanne disagreed. "This is anything but great."

"Wow, our first fight. This is so us. We're like an old married couple."

Roxanne needed to set Tighten straight. "Look,

84

there is no *us*, okay? There will never be an *us*!"

Tighten didn't understand. "But, I have powers . . . I have a cape. I'm the good guy!"

"You *are* a good guy, Hal. But you don't understand. We need to find out why Megamind did this to you."

This didn't make sense to Tighten. He was the hero now, and the hero always got the girl, right?

"Hal, just take a deep breath and listen to me for a moment," Roxanne said, trying to calm him down. "I'm trying to warn you, Hal."

"It's *Tighten*, not Hal." And with that, Tighten flew off like a speeding bullet, glass shattering from the side of the building behind him.

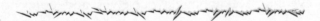

Meanwhile, Megamind was sitting at a table in a restaurant, waiting for his date to show up. Nervously, he glanced at his watch: Roxanne was late.

"Bernard!" Megamind heard Roxanne call out. His face brightened.

Roxanne raced over to the table, her hair a mess. She apologized for being late.

"Wow, your hair . . . looks exciting!" Megamind told her.

"That's not the only exciting development of the night," Roxanne said, lowering her voice. "Megamind created Tighten!"

Megamind gasped.

"It's kind of pathetic when you think about it," Roxanne said.

"Maybe he's met somebody that's altered his outlook on things," Megamind suggested. "He might be thinking of hanging up the whole villainy thing altogether."

"Why would he pick Hal?" Roxanne wondered. "Hal is the worst possible person you could pick. My mind is completely boggled."

"You know, what do you say, for the remainder of the evening, we unboggle ourselves and concentrate on something besides Megamind, heroes, and poor judgment? Like, I don't know . . . us?" Megamind suggested.

"I'm sorry, Bernard," Roxanne said. "Of course, you're right. I could use a breather."

Roxanne raised her glass. "To Bernard. For being the only normal thing in my crazy, upside-down world."

Megamind was stunned. No one had ever thought he was normal before. He raised his glass, too. "To being normal," he toasted.

Roxanne and Megamind were so lost in the moment that they didn't see Tighten watching them from outside the restaurant window. Tighten watched as the two laughed; they looked happy together. Tighten, on the other hand, was not happy at all.

Megamind cleared his throat. He needed to ask Roxanne a very important question. "Roxanne?" he started.

"Yes," she replied.

"Say I wasn't so normal," Megamind began. "Let's say I was bald and had a complexion of a popular primary color. As a random, nonspecific example. Would you still enjoy my company?"

"Of course," Roxanne answered with a smile. "You don't judge a book by its cover or a person from the outside."

Megamind exhaled. "Oh, that's a relief to hear."

"You judge them based on their actions," Roxanne continued.

"Well, that seems kind of petty, don't you think?" Megamind asked.

Roxanne laughed. The two locked eyes, then leaned in for a kiss! Roxanne touched his arm and accidentally touched Megamind's watch, turning off his disguise!

Suddenly, people in the restaurant began to scream. Roxanne, still locked in the kiss, opened her eyes to find that she was smooching with Megamind! Slapping the villain in the face, Roxanne gasped in horror.

"Don't look at me!" Megamind shouted. "It's just a technical glitch."

Frantically, he slapped at his watch.

And he turned into the warden!

"Don't look!" Megamind shouted again, hitting his watch again.

This time he turned into Space Dad!

"Now where were we?" Megamind said.

Roxanne threw a cup of water at him, and his Space Dad disguise fizzled away.

"You!" Roxanne shouted.

"Now, now, hold on . . . ," Megamind began.

"You!" Roxanne repeated as she raced from the restaurant.

As Roxanne ran home through the pouring rain, she heard a car skid to a stop next to her. Startled, she looked around, but didn't see anything. Then, moments later, Megamind popped out.

"I can explain," he told her.

Roxanne huffed and turned away. She did *not* want

to hear what the villain had to say.

Megamind followed her. "What about everything you just said? About judging a book by its cover?"

Roxanne stopped and faced Megamind. "Well, let's take a look at the contents, then, shall we? You destroyed Metro Man! You took over the city! And then, you actually got me to care about you! Why are you so evil? Tricking me? What could you possibly hope to gain?"

She stared at Megamind, who had a pained expression on his face. Wait a minute—could it be that this guy *actually* liked her?

"Do you really think that I would *ever* be with you?" Roxanne asked him.

"No," Megamind answered, hanging his head.

And with that, Roxanne walked off into the rainy night, leaving poor Megamind alone.

CHAPTER TWELVE

It was daylight by the time Megamind returned to his hideout.

"Minion!" he shouted, bursting through the door. "Okay, Minion, you were right. I was . . . less right. It's time to get back on track. You can come out now. Minion?"

Megamind listened to his voice echo through the empty halls. Then he remembered that Minion was gone, too. Megamind was truly alone.

Just then, the Brainbots scurried in. At least some *things* were left.

Megamind pointed to a Brainbot. "Bring out the Black Mamba," he commanded.

The Brainbots flew through a hallway and unlocked a glass display case with the words *The most frightening cape*

and collar ensemble the world has ever seen written on it. Quickly, the Brainbots dressed Megamind in evil-looking black boots and an even scarier-looking pair of black gloves. Then two Brainbots flew to Megamind's shoulders and draped a cape around his neck. And for the finishing touch, the Brainbots applied powder to his head and black eyeliner under his eyes.

Megamind stepped up to a cracked mirror and looked at his reflection. The transformation was complete!

Megamind looked over at his idea wall and scanned the steps from *Prepare to get Tighten* to *Robot* to step number ninety-one: *Fight Tighten*. He picked up a jelly doughnut and drew a circle around step number ninety-one. Then he held up the doughnut and crushed it!

With a swish of his cape, Megamind walked over to a large figure that was draped with a tarp. With dramatic flare, he ripped off the tarp and stared up at a huge robot.

"Okay, Tighten, it's time to go down with style," Megamind said out loud, climbing onto the robot. The robot sprung to life, imitating Megamind's every move.

From his perch on the robot's head, Megamind and the giant robot marched into Metro City. Police cars zoomed down the streets, their sirens blasting as the giant robot's feet smashed everything in its path.

"Citizens of Metrocity," Megamind's voice projected through giant speakers, "I hear there is a new hero who dares challenge my evil. Where is the one they call Tighten?"

The robot blasted off into the sky and landed on the top of City Hall.

"Where is this magnificent specimen of goodness that has stolen you hearts?" Megamind continued. "It's nine o'clock, let the showdown begin!"

Fireworks shot off of the robot as Megamind jumped down from the roof. He was ready to face off against Tighten. The only problem was that Tighten was nowhere to be seen!

Megamind and his robot waited and waited, but Tighten did not show up.

"Unprofessional!" Megamind declared. "That's what this is."

If Tighten wouldn't come to him, then Megamind would go to Tighten. Megamind rode the robot over to Tighten's apartment, and the robot punched a hole through the wall.

"Would Metro Man have kept me waiting?" Megamind asked Tighten. "Of course not. He was a pro."

Tighten barely looked up from the video game he

was playing. "Hey, Megamind! You're actually the guy I wanted to see. Also, there's a door here."

Megamind walked down the robot's arm and entered the apartment. "Do you have any idea how long I waited for you?"

"No, no, no, I totally understand what you're saying," Tighten told him. "Can you just shut up for one second? I'm trying to beat this level." And he turned back to his video game.

"Were you even planning on showing up?" Megamind asked.

"Well, at first I was going to, because, you know, that's what I figured I was supposed to do."

As Tighten spoke, Megamind looked around the apartment. And he was horrified at what he saw—ATMs, piles of cash, and all sorts of electronics! Tighten was a thief! But that was wrong—Tighten was supposed to be a *hero*.

"Being a hero is for losers," Tighten said. "It's work, work, work, 24/7. And for what?"

Tighten picked up a picture of Roxanne in Metro Man's arms. "I only took the gig to get the girls. And it turns out Roxanne doesn't want anything to do with me."

"Roxanne? Roxanne Ritchi?" Megamind asked.

"Yeah, Roxanne Ritchi," Tighten said. "I saw her having dinner and making googly eyes at some intellectual dweeb."

Megamind realized that Tighten must have been spying on him and Roxanne during their date. *Ooops!*

Then Tighten told Megamind that he thought the two of them should team up! With Tighten's power and Megamind's big-headedness, they could rule the city.

Megamind couldn't believe his ears. He and Tighten team up? That was ridiculous!

"I even drew up some new costume designs," Tighten said, showing him some drawings.

Megamind was dumbfounded. *Costume designs?*

"You'd be the brain, so you'd get a little brain on your costume, and I'll have the brawn on mine," Tighten explained.

"There's only one villain in this city, and that's me," Megamind declared. "I certainly don't need a partner."

"I was thinking you'd be more like my assistant," Tighten told him.

Megamind stared at him in disgust. "I can't believe you. All your gifts, all your powers, and you squander them for your own personal gain?"

"Yes!" Tighten agreed.

"No! I'm the villain. You're the good guy. I do something bad, and you come and get me. That's why I created you!" Megamind shouted.

"Yeah, right. You're nuts! Space Dad told me—" Tighten started.

Megamind pressed a button on his watch and was instantly transformed into Space Dad. "You should be more like Metro Man!" he said.

Tighten screamed as Megamind turned back into himself. Tighten couldn't believe he had been tricked!

Megamind saw that Tighten was getting upset. Maybe if he continued to taunt him, he'd be in the mood for a fight.

"I'm also the intellectual dweeb," Megamind said as he turned himself into Bernard.

"No," was all a shocked Tighten could say.

"And we were smooching up a storm," Megamind said, making a kissy face at Tighten.

Tighten's blood began to boil. "When I get my hands on you, I'm gonna—"

But Megamind didn't let him finish his sentence. He jumped onto the giant robot and backed away from the building. "Yes, yes, I know. Bring me to justice. Oh, how I've missed this."

Tighten flew out of the building and, with one mighty punch, sent Megamind and his robot flying through the streets.

"And the hero strikes the first blow!" Megamind cried. "But evil returns with a backhand."

Megamind punched Tighten and Tighten landed hard on the ground. He looked back at Megamind, who was laughing at him.

Tighten wasn't about to go down without more of a fight. He let out a growl and flung himself forward. He flew through the air in search of Megamind.

But Megamind and his robot were hiding behind a tall building. They watched as Tighten flew past them.

"Come out, you little freak!" Tighten called as he hovered in midair. "I want to see what that big brain looks like on the pavement!"

Just then, the robot snuck up behind Tighten and tapped him on the shoulder. As Tighten spun around, the robot punched him into a building. *Bam!* Tighten's head smashed right through the building's wall. With a snarl, Tighten pulled his head out. Megamind just laughed and walked away.

"You fell for the oldest evil trick in the book," he said.

"You little blue twerp!" Tighten, who had fully recovered, called after Megamind. He zoomed ahead and flew around a corner. *Bang!* Megamind hit Tighten with a lamppost.

"En garde!" Megamind called.

Quickly, Tighten snatched up a second lamppost and the two started "sword" fighting in the middle of the city.

"Now that's the spirit!" Megamind called as he swung his weapon. "Parry, thrust, parry again." He called out sword fighting moves. "Now, it's time for some witty back-and-forth banter. You go first," he told Tighten.

"Aaahhh!" was Tighten's response.

"Okay . . . not sure where to go with that," Megamind said.

"This one's for stealing my girlfriend," Tighten responded as he swung his lamppost.

The blow sent Megamind and the robot into the air.

Tighten flew up after him. "This one's for Space Dad making a fool out of me," he said, pushing the robot back down toward the city.

"Aaahhh!" Megamind cried out.

Tighten was really angry now and showing his true strength. He pushed Megamind and the robot through several stories of a building. They landed hard on the ground.

"Well done!" Megamind said, looking out from the robot. "I thought the battle went really, really well. I mean, I have a few notes—"

"Notes?!" Tighten interrupted. What was Megamind talking about?

"But they can wait," Megamind continued. He held up his arms to be handcuffed. "Okay, you can take me to jail now."

Tighten shook his head. "Oh, no, no, no. I was thinking more like the morgue. You're dead."

Megamind held up his hand. "*Whoa, whoa, whoa . . .* this isn't how you play the game."

"Game over!" Tighten declared.

Megamind started to get nervous. This guy was serious—he *really* wanted to kill him! Megamind was certain that his life was really in danger this time.

Tighten cocked his fist back. He was ready to deliver the final death blow.

"*Aaahhh!*" Megamind screamed.

Panicked, Megamind hit the eject button. Immediately, he was thrown from the robot, soared through the air, and was caught by two Brainbots. The

Brainbots flew Megamind through the streets, with Tighten in hot pursuit.

"Okay, I'm calling a time-out. Time-out! Time-out!" Megamind shouted as the Brainbots tried to carry him to safety.

The Brainbots flew through traffic as fast as they could. Suddenly, they spotted a truck up ahead—and it was coming straight toward them. At the last moment, they swerved to avoid a crash. *Boom!* Tighten, who had been at their heels, hit the truck head-on. The force of the explosion made the Brainbots crash, and Megamind went skidding across the street.

Groaning in pain, Megamind looked up. Tighten was coming toward him—and he did *not* look happy.

"Brainbots," Megamind whispered into his watch, "initiate the fail-safe!"

Just as Tighten was almost on top of Megamind, two Brainbots dropped a copper dome over him. Tighten was trapped.

"Guess what, Buster Brown!" an elated (and relieved) Megamind shouted. "It's made from copper. You're powerless against it. It's the very same material used to defeat—"

Crash!

Tighten's fist easily punched through the copper.

"Metro Man?" Megamind continued.

Tighten tore himself out of the dome, and stared down at Megamind. "You should stop comparing me to Metro Man."

And with that, Tighten hurled the dome at Megamind. Megamind ran and jumped behind a building, just narrowly escaping.

"You can run, Megamind, but you can't hide!" Tighten called.

Huge crowds gathered and cheered for Tighten. He was their new hero, or was he?

"We're free! We are free!" the mayor shouted, happy that there was finally someone to stand up to Megamind.

"Oh, I wouldn't say free," Tighten told the mayor. "More like . . . under new management." And with a flick of his finger, he sent the mayor flying.

"What are you looking at?" Tighten asked the crowd that had gathered.

The crowd scattered, screaming as they ran.

Who was this guy, they wondered. He was supposed to be their hero, but a hero wouldn't act that way—would he?

CHAPTER THIRTEEN

When Megamind was certain he had lost Tighten, he relaxed. But just for a moment. The hero he had created was nuts. This wasn't how the game was supposed to be played. Megamind had to turn to someone, but who? Minion had left him, and Roxanne never wanted to see him again. Roxanne. Hmm . . . it was worth a shot.

Megamind and his Brainbots headed over to Roxanne's apartment and rang the bell. Luckily, the reporter opened the door.

"Tighten's turned evil," Megamind said as he rushed inside.

"So you came here to hide?" Roxanne asked.

Just then, they heard a voice from outside. "I'm gonna tear this city apart until you come out!" It was Tighten! And he was desperate to find Megamind. Megamind quickly shut the windows and blinds.

"I just need some more of Metro Man's DNA," Megamind explained to Roxanne. He thought that Roxanne might have some of it around her place—a lock of Metro Man's hair, perhaps?

Roxanne didn't understand. If Megamind had given Tighten his powers, then why couldn't he just take them away?

But Megamind couldn't do that. He had misplaced his invisible car the night Roxanne dumped him. And what was in the car? The Infuser Gun! Without the Infuser Gun, he couldn't turn Tighten back into Hal.

Megamind walked over to the window and opened the blinds. Roxanne walked over next to him and looked outside. Down below, Metro City was a mess—buildings were burning, cars had crashed—the place was on the brink of ruin.

"Isn't that what you always wanted?" Roxanne asked. "You used to love terrorizing the city. Why the sudden change now? Because you're not the one doing it?"

"All I wanted was to put things back the way they were—when there was good in the world, when Metro Man was still alive," Megamind told her. "I've made a mess of things, Roxanne. I just need to fix this."

"I don't have anything," Roxanne said.

Megamind hung his head. Seeing this, Roxanne softened a bit. Maybe Megamind wasn't so bad, after all. She wished she could help him, but she didn't have anything of Metro Man's. Then she had an idea.

"We could always try his place."

"*His* place? Megamind asked. That was it—Roxanne knew where the hero used to live.

Megamind and Roxanne got into the news van and drove away from the destroyed city. They drove past a dead-end sign on a secluded mountain road, and continued until they came to a little red schoolhouse.

"This is it," Roxanne announced.

Megamind was shocked. It was the same little red schoolhouse he and Metro Man had attended when they were boys, the same one that Megamind had tried to destroy. "So, this is where he hid it."

Megamind and Roxanne entered the building and walked down a long, tall corridor.

"Wow, I don't remember it being so big on the inside," Megamind commented.

"You know," Roxanne started, "I think there's an apology in order for the other night."

"Okay, that would be nice but make it quick. We have

much more pressing matters to deal with," Megamind told her.

"I meant an apology from you!" Roxanne exclaimed.

"Oh, oh, right," Megamind said.

Megamind and Roxanne reached a door and opened it. Megamind couldn't believe his eyes—the walls were covered with photographs, news articles, and other memorabilia of their battles over the years. Megamind was shocked that Metro Man had actually kept all that stuff.

"What should I be looking for?" Roxanne wanted to know.

"Anything. Dandruff. A lock of his hair, chewed gum. A half-eaten sandwich," Megamind listed.

"Well, I'll start looking in here," Roxanne said, walking into Metro Man's dressing room.

"There was always that mutual respect between us," Megamind said, his eyes filling with tears.

Inside the dressing room, Roxanne looked around. Suddenly, she found something—a single strand of hair. She called out for Megamind and showed him what she had discovered.

Megamind rushed into the room wearing Metro Man's old cape. Stumbling over the cape, he tripped and fell, landing at Roxanne's feet.

Then, seeing the strand of hair, he picked it up and said, "Fantastic, this will be just enough to create a new hero."

Just then, they heard the buzz of a power tool and laughter. It was coming from somewhere inside Metro Man's schoolhouse. Suddenly, a secret door opened. And in walked Metro Man reading a newspaper and shaving his face with an electric sander!

Metro Man was alive!

CHAPTER FOURTEEN

"You're alive?" a stunned Roxanne asked.

"You're alive?" an equally stunned Megamind echoed.

"I'm alive," Metro Man confirmed.

Roxanne couldn't believe it. After all, they had seen Metro Man's skeleton. In her mind he was 100 percent dead!

Megamind was still in shock. He reached out to touch Metro Man's cheek. "Are you a ghost?"

"Okay, it all started back at the observatory," Metro Man started to explain. "While we were still bickering."

He went on to tell them that on the day Megamind kidnapped Roxanne (again), the plan was for him to stop Megamind (again). But something was wrong; his head wasn't really in the game. He realized that they had played the same silly game so many times that the challenge was gone. He knew how this one would end—he'd rescue Roxanne, and once again be the hero.

"I began to realize that despite all my powers, each and every citizen of Metro City had something I didn't—a choice," Metro Man said.

Megamind and Roxanne listened carefully to what he was saying. It was true. Metro Man only had one role to play—that of a hero.

"But what about what I wanted to do?" Metro Man asked. "Then it suddenly hit me. What am I doing with my life? No one said this hero thing had to be a lifetime gig. But you can't just quit, either. That's when I got the brilliant idea to fake my death."

So Metro Man just *pretended* that his weakness was copper. Then, using his super speed, he flew off to a nearby nursing school and borrowed a skeleton! And when the real observatory was hit by the Death Ray beam and exploded, Metro Man threw the skeleton toward the fake observatory.

"Metro Man was finally dead," Metro Man concluded. "And Music Man was born," he added.

"Music Man?" a confused Roxanne asked.

Metro Man flashed his shiny, white teeth. "That way I can keep my logo," he joked. "I was finally free to get in touch with the only thing that has ever truly challenged me . . . the music! That's my true power. Weaving lyrical magic. Check this out."

And with that, Metro Man began to sing.

"You're horrible," Roxanne said, covering her ears.

"Granted, you have talent," Megamind said, trying to change the subject, "but there's a madman out there destroying our—your city."

Metro Man shrugged. "You know what I call a madman destroying the city? Thursday. Let someone else handle it."

Roxanne was furious. "How can you do this? The people of this city relied on you and you deserted them. You left us in the hands of him!" she said, pointing to Megamind. "No offense," she added.

Megamind shook his head. He wasn't offended. In fact, he totally agreed with Roxanne. They needed Metro Man's help!

"People just take heroes for granted. I'm done with the whole game," Metro Man told them.

"*La, la, la,*" Metro Man sang. "I've moved on. You should, too."

Megamind was deflated. It was no use—Metro Man was out of the game.

It was over. Megamind and Roxanne said good-bye and left Metro Man alone with his music.

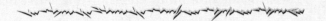

Megamind and Roxanne climbed up a hill and stood there looking down at the city. They needed time to think.

"Well, at least we got what we came for," Roxanne said, motioning toward the strand of Metro Man's hair that Megamind was carrying. "We can do it on our own."

Suddenly, Megamind let go of the hair.

Roxanne was stunned. What was Megamind doing? They needed the hair to get Metro Man's DNA. And they needed the DNA to create another hero—a *real* hero. Now what were they going to do?

"It was a stupid plan," Megamind told her. "They've all been stupid plans."

Roxanne didn't understand. "So that's it? You're just giving up?"

Megamind turned to face the reporter. "Did you hear that in there? My entire criminal career has been a joke. With me as the punch line. I could never defeat Metro Man. How could I possibly defeat Tighten?"

"But you never give up," Roxanne insisted. "Even

when you have absolutely no chance of winning. It's your best quality. You need to be that guy now."

"Then you might want to find someone with a better batting average," Megamind told her. "I'm the bad guy. I lose. I always lose."

"Like it or not, the city needs your help," Roxanne stated. "We don't need any more bad guys. What we need right now is a hero."

Megamind shook his head. "Don't you get it? There are no heroes, Roxanne. No real ones, anyway."

"You're wrong about that," Roxanne told him.

"I'm going home. Where I belong," Megamind declared.

And with that, he turned around and left.

CHAPTER FIFTEEN

Megamind knew where he belonged—in prison. And that's exactly where he went. He was a villain, after all, and villains didn't belong on the streets. No, villains belonged behind bars. Megamind went directly to the Metro City Penitentary and held out his wrists. The warden immediately cuffed him and led him inside.

Meanwhile, Tighten was busy destroying the city. People were running, scared for their lives. Cars and buildings had been cut in half. Police sirens wailed through the streets. Nothing could stop Tighten. He was determined to destroy everything in his path.

And although Roxanne Ritchi was still disappointed that Megamind wouldn't play the part of the hero, she still thought there was something she could do to stop Tighten. She jumped into her van and drove around until she spotted Tighten. He was standing on a construction crane.

"Hal!" Roxanne called up to him, running out of the van.

"Let me guess," Tighten said, flying down to her side. "After seeing how awesome I am, you've finally come to your senses. Well, it's too late. I'm over you."

"I've come to stop you, Hal," Roxanne declared.

"You?" Tighten was amused. "Oh, wow, what're you gonna do? Report me to death?"

"I was going to try reasoning with you," Roxanne told him. "You and I, we worked together a long time. I know you."

"You don't know me," Tighten scoffed. "You never took the time to know me. This is the first time we've hung out socially and it's when I'm about to destroy the city."

"I want to talk to the real Hal," Roxanne said. "I want to talk to the guy who loved being a cameraman, and eating dip, and being a nerd, and being not as scary as the Tighten Hal."

"Too late!" Tighten shouted.

"It's not too late. I know there's some good in you somewhere," Roxanne said.

But Tighten wasn't going to listen to her. He wasn't good—he was pure evil through and through, and he liked it that way!

"You're so naïve, Roxie," Tighten said. "You see the good in everybody even when it's not there. You're living a fantasy. There is no Easter bunny, there is no tooth fairy, and there is no Queen of England." (Actually, there *is* a Queen of England, but that's besides the point—let's get on with the story . . .)

"This is the real world," Tighten continued. "You need to wake up."

And with that, he lifted the news van over his head, shook out a camera, and tossed the van over his shoulder.

Roxanne wasn't about to give up. "Good will always defeat evil," she told him.

"Well, let's put your theory to the test," Tighten responded, lifting the camera to his face.

Back at Metro City Penitentiary, Megamind was kicking back and watching a little TV. As he flipped through the channels, Tighten's face filled the screen. Megamind put down the remote and stared at the television.

"Megamind!" Tighten shouted. "You and I have some unfinished business. I'll be waiting at Metro City Tower."

And as an added warning, Tighten pointed the camera at his hostage, Roxanne Ritchi. She was tied up, a look of sheer exhaustion on her face.

"Roxanne!" Megamind shouted.

"Come on, Roxie. Call for your *hero* to come rescue you," Tighten threatened.

But Roxie wouldn't call out. She knew that Megamind had left and she doubted that he was even listening. Like Metro Man, Megamind was done playing the game.

Tighten tried again to get Roxanne to call out for Megamind, and again she refused. "There are no heroes anymore. No real ones, anyway," Roxanne said.

Seeing the hopelessness in Roxanne's face, Megamind's heart sank.

"You have one hour," Tighten addressed Megamind. "Don't keep me waiting."

And with that, Tighten cut off the transmission.

"Roxanne," Megamind said out loud. He *had* to get out of prison! He *had* to rescue Roxanne.

Megamind rushed to his cell door and pressed his face against the window. "Warden! Listen to me. You have to let me go! Tighten has to be stopped."

The warden appeared in the window. "Sorry, Megamind, you still have eighty-eight life sentences to go. Plenty of time to reflect on what you've done."

Megamind was desperate. So desperate in fact that he *apologized*!

But the warden didn't buy Megamind's apology.

"I don't blame you," Megamind told him. "I've terrorized the city countless times. I created a hero who's turned out to be a villain. I lied to Roxanne. My best friend, Minion, I treated like dirt. But, please, don't make this city—don't make Roxanne—pay for my wrongdoings."

Suddenly, the cell door opened. "Apology accepted," the warden said.

Megamind was shocked. Could it be that he was actually being set free?

Then, the warden looked down at his watch, pressed a button, and turned into Minion!

The warden was really Minion the entire time! Minion was just waiting for a personal apology. Satisfied, Minion beckoned Megamind to go.

As the pair walked out of the penitentiary, they passed the real warden, who was tied up in a corner.

"Good luck, fellas!" the warden called from under his gag. Apparently, the real warden was on Megamind's side, too!

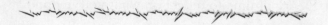

Back at Metro City Tower, Tighten was looking around for any sign of Megamind. "Well, looks like your boyfriend ain't coming," he told Roxanne. "That's too bad. Well, it's time for the wrap-up," he said, turning the television camera toward himself.

"Hey, Metro losers," Tighten said into the camera. "This is Metro City Tower. They say it's supposed to be a symbol of our city's strength. But for me, it's a reminder of the day this woman ferociously ripped out my heart," he said, referring to Roxanne.

Then, throwing the camera over his shoulder and glaring evilly at Roxanne, he said, "Out of sight, out of mind."

And with that, he flew to the bottom of Metro City Tower and began cutting into the building's base. Glass shattered as it fell to the ground. The tower leaned to one side, almost knocking Roxanne from the top.

"Hal, you don't have to do this!" Roxanne called down to him.

"My entire life, I've failed at everything," Tighten said. "It turns out being bad is the only thing I've ever been good at."

Suddenly, loud music began playing around them. Dark clouds rolled in. Lasers blasted.

"You dare challenge me?" Megamind's voice sounded.

"This town isn't big enough for two super-villains," Tighten said.

"You're a villain, all right," Megamind agreed. "Just not a super one."

"Yeah? What's the difference?" Tighten wanted to know.

"Presentation," Megamind stated.

And with that, a huge swarm of Brainbots flew out of the dark cloud and formed the shaped of Megamind's head. The giant head opened its mouth and swallowed Tighten!

Suddenly, the tower began to fall with Roxanne still on top of it! But at the last moment, Megamind swooped in on a hoverjet and untied her.

"I assume you have a plan?" Roxanne asked Megamind.

"Well, that was the plan," Megamind told her. "Now, I'm just kinda winging it."

Tighten focused his gaze on the Brainbots and shot a deadly laser out of his eyes. *Boom!* All of the Brainbots were destroyed. With the Brainbots out of the way,

Tighten could now focus on getting Megamind and Roxanne. He picked up the tower and hurled it in their direction.

Seeing the huge building flying toward him, Megamind punched the gas on his hoverjet. But it was no use—he knew he couldn't outrun the tower. Desperate, he tossed Roxanne to safety on a nearby building awning. Moments later, the building hit his hoverjet, sending him flying through the air.

Roxanne looked up from her safe spot, only to see Megamind lying motionless by the fountain in the town square.

"No!" Roxanne called out in despair.

"Well, that was easy," Tighten said, landing in the town square. "Looks like there's only one loose end now."

And with that, the hero-turned-villain kicked a crashed bus toward Roxanne.

Roxanne cowered in fear as the bus hurtled in her direction. But before the bus made impact, it split in half. Someone had saved her life, but who?

Metro Man!

"Please, let's have a little respect for public transportation," Metro Man told Tighten.

Roxanne couldn't believe her eyes. "You came back."

"You were right, Roxanne. I never should have left," Metro Man told her.

"Well, I, I thought you were dead," a nervous Tighten said.

"My death was greatly exaggerated," Metro Man explained. "So, you're the punk I've heard about," he continued, flexing his muscles and taking a step toward Tighten.

Tighten gulped, and then took off like a shot! But Metro Man was right on his heels.

As Metro Man took off in pursuit of Tighten, Roxanne ran over to Megamind. She was desperate to find out how badly he was hurt.

"I'm sorry. I did the best I could," Megamind mumbled.

"I'm so proud of you," Roxanne said.

Just then, Roxanne heard an electrical popping sound and Megamind was transformed into Minion!

"Minion?" a confused Roxanne asked.

"Surprise. I'm the real hero," Minion said weakly. All that was left of him was his fish head in its cracked and empty fishbowl.

If this was Minion, then where in the world was Megamind? Roxanne scanned the sky for a glimpse of him, but all she could see was Metro Man chasing Tighten.

Wait a minute—that wasn't Metro Man up there, it was Megamind in disguise!

Desperate to escape, Tighten threw pieces of buildings in Metro Man's path, but the hero easily avoided them. Then Tighten picked up a car and hurled it behind him. As he looked up, he saw Metro Man strolling toward him.

"Going somewhere?" Metro Man asked. "Besides jail?"

Tighten turned a corner and crashed right into Metro Man. Roxanne watched as the hero grabbed Tighten and pulled his fist back for a mighty punch.

"Not in the face, man," Tighten said, cowering.

Metro Man lowered his fist. "Get out of Metrocity, Tighten. Or you'll answer to me."

"You got it," Tighten told him as he quickly flew from the city.

Satisfied that Tighten was gone, Metro Man flew back to the town square. There, he was greeted by a cheering crowd.

"It's you, isn't it?" Roxanne asked the hero.

Metro Man smiled and winked at her.

Suddenly, Roxanne saw Tighten standing behind Megamind/Metro Man. The villain was back!

"Wait a second," Tighten said.

Metro Man spun around.

"Metrocity?" Tighten said. "There's only one person I know who calls this town Metrocity."

"I didn't say *Metrocity*," Megamind/Metro Man shot back. "I said *Met-ROH-city*. Anyway, I'm Metro Man, and you're really trying my patience."

"If you're Metro Man, then why are you afraid of me?" Tighten asked.

"I'm not," Megamind/Metro Man said.

"Then why do you keep backing away?" Tighten wanted to know.

"Just getting some fighting room," Megamind/Metro Man told him.

Tighten focused his eyes on Megamind/Metro Man and let loose a series of deadly lasers. Frantically, Megamind/Metro Man dodged the blasts. But one laser blew up a car, and the blast sent Megamind/Metro Man to the ground.

As he lay there, crumpled in a heap, Megamind/ Metro Man looked at the debris around him. This was it—he had lost the final battle. But wait, what did he see over there? It was debris, but it was moving. And it was in the outline of his invisible car. Maybe all hope wasn't lost yet.

Just then, the disguise generator sparked, and Metro Man was changed back into Megamind with a Brainbot strapped to his back.

"I knew it!" a furious Tighten exclaimed. He lifted Megamind up by his collar. "This is the last time you make a fool out of me."

"I made you a hero. You did the fool thing all by yourself," Megamind told him.

Upon hearing that, Tighten punched Megamind, sending him sailing across the street. *Bang!* Megamind landed hard against a building.

"Any final words, Blue Man?" Tighten taunted.

"Just some advice. A lesson I learned over the years," Megamind said as he inched toward his invisible car.

As Megamind painfully pulled himself up, he saw Roxanne running up behind Tighten. He motioned for her to stay away.

"Would you like to hear it?" Megamind asked Tighten.

"Oh yeah, what's that?" Tighten answered.

"Good always defeats evil," Megamind declared.

And before Tighten could respond, Megamind lunged forward and jumped into the backseat of his invisible car. Tighten stood there, dumbfounded, as Megamind seemingly disappeared into thin air!

Megamind flipped the switch on the Infuser Gun to reverse. Looking frantically for Megamind, Tighten managed to rip off the door of the invisible car. Perfect— Megamind had the villain exactly where he wanted him!

Megamind stuck the Infuser Gun up Tighten's nose and pulled the trigger. In an instant, Tighten was transformed back into Hal and fell unconscious to the ground.

Exhausted, Megamind climbed out of the car and looked down at his fallen enemy.

"I knew you'd come back," Roxanne said, running up to him.

"Well, that made one of us," Megamind said.

Roxanne looked back over her shoulder. "He's been asking for you," she said, nodding at Minion.

Megamind raced over to his friend, and knelt down.

"Who is it?" Minion asked weakly. "I can't see, it's cold and warm, and dark and light."

"It's me, Minion. I'm right here," Megamind told him.

"We've had a lot of adventures together, you and I," Minion said.

"Yes, Minion, we have."

Minion gave a weak cough. "I mean, most of them ended in horrible failure, but we won today, didn't we, sir?"

Megamind nodded. "Yes, Minion. Thanks in no small part to you."

"For good. For evil," Minion struggled to say. "It is my gr . . . well, let's be honest, it *was* my great honor to be your lackey, sir. Oh, I think this is it . . . I'm going far aw . . ." Minion twitched and closed his eyes. Then he was still.

"What a drama queen," Megamind scoffed as he picked Minion up out of his fishbowl and threw him into the fountain.

Minion opened his eyes. "You know, I'm feeling much better now."

And with that, the fish jumped around in the fountain. "I guess I just needed a swim."

A few feet away, Hal began to wake up. "I just had the strangest dream," he said.

Hal yawned and stretched and then he heard a clicking sound. He looked up and saw two cops snapping handcuffs on his wrists.

"Wait, wait, it wasn't me!" Hal protested. "It was opposite me! His name is Nat-it."

"You did it! You won!" an elated Roxanne Ritchi shouted, ignoring Hal and focusing her attention on Megamind.

"He did it! He did it!" an equally happy Minion spouted from the fountain.

"I did it. I did it!" Megamind echoed.

A crowd had gathered around Megamind. And they, too, were equally happy.

Suddenly, Roxanne threw her arms around Megamind. He really *had* done it—he'd saved the city *and* gotten the girl. He hugged Roxanne back.

"I did it! I did it! I did it!" Megamind shouted over and over.

The crowd cheered and tried to lift their new hero in the air. Panicking, Megamind drew up his Dehydration Gun. The crowd cowered.

Gently, Roxanne lowered his arm. "Sorry, he's just not used to positive feedback," she told the crowd.

Everyone drew in a big sigh of relief. Tighten was gone, and Megamind had changed from villain to hero. Things in Metro City were beginning to look up!

EPILOGUE

And that, my friends is the story. A story of good and evil. A story of evil turning good. A story with a happy ending.

Some time after my victory, the mayor of Metro City invited me to a ceremony at the museum. I have to admit, being good has its perks.

It was a ribbon-cutting ceremony and I used my Dehydration Gun to snap the thing in two. A multistory curtain dropped, revealing a statue of—who else?—me!

Funny, I guess destiny is not the path given to us, but the path we choose for ourselves. As long as there is evil, good will always stand against it.

Megamind: Defender of Metro City. You know, I like the sound of that.

THE END